Total-E-Bound Publishing books by Cassidy Ryan:

Bound by Love
Aria
Cadence
Imperfect

TRUTH AND BEAUTY

CASSIDY RYAN

Truth and Beauty
ISBN # 978-0-85715-995-3
©Copyright Cassidy Ryan 2012
Cover Art by Lyn Taylor ©Copyright April 2012
Interior text design by Claire Siemaszkiewicz
Total-E-Bound Publishing

TRUTH AND BEAUTY

Dedication

For my wonderful beta readers, Josie and Janalyn;
your honesty and encouragement kept me going.

Chapter One

In the space of half a heartbeat, Alex Jennings went from sound asleep to wide awake, eyes darting around the room, hands clutching at the bed as a sound like the loudest thunder he had ever heard rumbled through the house. The glass light fixture over the bed rattled and the pile of coins he'd stacked on the bedside table the night before tipped over, spilling over the table and onto the hardwood floor.

When the shock of his rude awakening started to subside, and his heart rate had returned to something resembling normal, a scowl pulled Alex's eyebrows together. Pushing the covers aside, he swung his legs over the side of the bed, got to his feet and moved quickly over the cool floor out into the hallway and down the stairs, cursing darkly under his breath.

The rumbling—*banging*—got louder as he approached his father's office at the back of the house, and just as Alex shoved the door open there was an ear-splitting crash. Dear God, he felt like he had been on a three-day bender. He had to get a place of his own *soon*. It was fast becoming clear to him that living with one's parents when one was over thirty was nothing less than a shortcut to the mad house.

"Dad?" When there was no response, Alex cursed again and reluctantly moved further into the room. "Dad!"

Seated behind the drum kit, Robert Jennings was grinning like a loon, sweat dampening his thinning, sandy blond hair, arms flailing like he was having some kind of seizure. Robert's body jolted every time one of the sticks in his hands made contact with the drums, and when the cymbals made another discordant, screaming crash, a small grunt of pleasure that was—to Alex at least—quite disturbing, escaped his dad.

Alex moved to stand right in front of the drums, grimacing at the way the floor trembled under his feet and the noise reverberated through him. He could practically feel it bouncing off his bones and liquidising his organs.

"Dad!" Even at the top of his voice, Alex could barely hear himself over the cacophony, but his dad finally opened his eyes and, after taking a moment to focus, his grin became even wider.

"Alex! What do you think? Sounding good, right?" Robert made no move to stop, but actually seemed to pick up the tempo.

Fearing for his long-term hearing, Alex made a slicing motion with his hand across his throat. Robert stopped drumming so suddenly that the silence nearly knocked Alex on to his backside.

"Something I can do for you, son?" Robert's hands were still moving, tapping the drumsticks together almost absently, as if he'd forgotten how to remain still.

"Dad, it's barely eight o'clock in the morning. Do you have to do that *right now*?" Alex's ears were throbbing like he'd spent a night clubbing.

"I've got to practice." Robert Jennings, sixty-two-year-old former dentist, sounded like a sullen teenager.

Dragging a hand through his hair, Alex stared incredulously at the man who had once been so...*sane*. "For what, Dad? Are The Who holding auditions?"

"Dude, you're harshing my buzz." Robert spun one of the drumsticks between his fingers in a way that, if Alex hadn't been so dumbfounded, he would probably have found pretty impressive.

As it was, his jaw dropped and he sputtered, sounding like he was being strangled. "Harshing...what? *Dude*? What the fu..." He managed to cut off the curse before it fully formed, because, even though the man across from him was acting like someone Alex would cross the street to avoid, he was still his dad.

"Don't the neighbours ever complain?" When he was a child growing up on this street, all it had taken for the residents to work up a head of steam was a boisterous game of hide and seek. Alex found it incredible that they weren't threatening his dad with legal action at least for the seismic racket that must be emanating from the house.

Robert shook his head, and, grin returning, executed a drum roll that Alex felt in his teeth.

"These old houses are pretty solid, and, even if they weren't, everyone around here will be on their way to work by now." He was practically glowing with the smug satisfaction of the recently retired.

Alex shook his head and turned towards the door. "Can you just...try not to bring the house down?" He pulled the door closed behind him and got two steps down the hall before the floor started to rumble under his feet again. Knowing that there wasn't a chance in hell that he was going to get any more sleep, Alex headed to the kitchen to make himself some coffee.

As the percolator dripped and gurgled, he went to stand in front of the window and a smile tugged at the corners of his mouth. Out in the back garden his mother was scattering some kind of grain for the chickens pecking at her feet. Chickens. Alex shook his head again. Was it even legal to keep livestock in residential London? The neighbours must think his parents had both gone stark raving bonkers.

Turning away to take a mug from the cupboard, Alex picked up the phone when it rang and tucked it between his ear and shoulder as he poured his coffee.

"Hello?"

"Jennings, you bastard. I know where you are."

Laughter bubbled up in Alex and a wide smile curled his mouth. "Damian! How the hell are you?" He added sugar to his coffee and took the mug over to sit at the table.

"I'm pissed off with you, is how I am. You've been back nearly a month and I had to find out from that arsehole Andy Rowan!" Damian Stanhope didn't sound pissed off — Alex could hear the smile in his best friend's voice.

"Sorry, man, I was going to call you when I got my head on straight. The only reason Andy Rowan knows I'm back is because my mum's friends with his mum." Alex sipped on his coffee, slouching back with a soft sigh when his dad took a break from the drumming. He didn't add that he just hadn't been fit for company, and had been virtually a hermit since stepping over his parents' threshold.

"So, how was Africa?" Damian's voice sounded a little rough, like he'd only recently woken up himself.

Alex caught a glimpse of his mum outside, laughing as she dodged the chickens, and thought about his dad's manic expression as he beat out his dissonant rhythm.

"Sane," he replied, taking another sip of his coffee. *Mostly*, an inner voice supplied, but Alex slammed the door on it.

"Sane? Okay. I expected life-altering, enlightening, or even just hot, but I suppose sane is good." Alex couldn't help laughing at the confusion in his friend's voice.

He hooked his foot around the leg of another chair and dragged it out so that he could prop his feet up on it. "It's a long story. Suffice it to say, I'm staying with my folks and they're a little...changed since I went away."

"Changed? You mean physically, like surgically? Or changed like the pod people in that film? Because, you know, I've suspected for a few years now that my father might be a pod person." In his mind, Alex could picture the amusement lighting Damian's blue eyes, and for a second he *really* wanted to see his friend.

Alex laughed and warmth bloomed in him. "Actually, I wouldn't rule out the pod people theory. You know they both took early retirement? Well, Dad has taken up the drums—he looks like a demented octopus and sounds like he's rolling an oil drum full of bricks down a hill."

The sound of Damian's laughter stirred something inside Alex, something long dormant. Something that could not be allowed to re-awaken.

Quickly shaking it off before it had time to take hold, Alex continued. "You can laugh—you don't have to live with it. And as for Mum, she's gone all born-again hippy. She thinks they need to be more ecological or self-sufficient or some shit, and is growing *things* in the garden and raising chickens."

Damian snorted loudly. "*Things*?"

"There's something that looks a bit like carrots — twisted, mutant carrots — there might be tomatoes and I'm pretty sure she's got a few marijuana plants in the greenhouse, but it could be parsley." Alex got to his feet and went back to the coffee pot to refill his mug.

"Sounds like you're having a blast." Damian was clearly enjoying Alex's misfortunes.

Alex grinned. "It's a laugh a minute. So, what about you? What have you been up to?"

There was a long silence, and, when he finally replied, Damian's voice was low; tired sounding. "Oh, you know, the usual — working, travelling for work, getting divorced."

In the process of lifting his mug, Alex set it back down on the worktop with a *thunk* that sent hot liquid sloshing over the rim. He pulled his hand back just in time to avoid getting burnt.

"Divorced? *Again*? Damn, this is becoming a habit with you. You've barely been married two years this time. Isn't the third time supposed to be lucky or a charm or something?" Absently tearing some paper towel off the roll, Alex cleaned up his mess and leant back against the worktop.

Damian moaned, and Alex could picture him dragging his hand through his dark blond hair, a sheepish expression on his face.

"Shannon was a mistake from the start. Why didn't you warn me she was a manipulative, money-grabbing she-demon?" There was no heat in Damian's demand.

"How the hell should I have known what she was like when you didn't?" Okay, he hadn't liked Shannon all that much, but he hadn't been particularly keen on Gayle either, and Imogen had only grown on him *after* the divorce. Alex had always attributed his indifference to Damian's wives to his own feelings for his friend. Feelings that were kept locked tightly away, and were never ever to be spoken of.

"Aren't you supposed to be in touch with your feminine side or something?" Amusement was evident in Damian's voice.

Alex bit back his own smile. "You do understand that I'm gay and not actually a woman, right?"

"Okay, princess, don't get your knickers in a twist." Damian was clearly having difficulty containing his laughter, as little snorts and snickers leaked out.

"Are you trying to get your arse kicked, Stanhope?" Picking up his mug, Alex went back to sit at the table.

Damian made a *pfft* sound. "Yeah, yeah, you can try when you get here, Doc."

Surprised, Alex's eyebrows lifted and the mug halted halfway to his mouth. "When I get there?"

"We're having a bit of a bash at the weekend. You should come; it'll be fun." Pleasure swelled in Alex at the eagerness in his friend's voice, and acceptance was almost automatic. But another glimpse of his mum in the garden stayed his reply.

"I should probably stick around here for a while, spend some time with my folks, you know?" He felt a small stab of guilt at the knowledge that he would rather be with Damian than his own parents.

Damian paused long enough for Alex to feel his friend's disappointment. "Uh, sure, of course. But we'll get together soon, yes?"

"Oh yeah, definitely. Soon." Feeling suddenly deflated, Alex ended the call and slumped in his chair.

He looked up when the back door opened and his mum came in, bringing with her a blast of cool air. Alex shivered and wished he was wearing more than just his boxers.

"Good morning, love. You're up early." Beth dropped a kiss on his temple and went to the sink to wash her hands. "So, I was thinking about getting a goat. I hear goat's milk is very good for the skin. I'm going to speak to the man at the city zoo about it. He has a single gay son too," she added, with what he assumed was an attempt at casual.

A slow-building rumble from the direction of the office made Alex flinch. He set his mug down on the table and got to his feet.

"Mum, I'm going to head up to Damian's place for a while. You don't mind, do you? Okay, great." He left the kitchen before his mum could argue, and headed up stairs that trembled unsettlingly under his feet as his dad built to an earthquake-inducing crescendo.

Chapter Two

Making no attempt to stifle a jaw-cracking yawn, Damian stumbled down the stairs, scratching his stomach and rubbing his stubble-roughened jaw in what he considered to be a show of remarkable coordination, given that he couldn't quite manage to force his eyes all the way open. At the bottom of the stairs he winced when he moved from thick, soft carpet on to cool, hardwood floor, bare toes curling involuntarily.

"Well, if it isn't Little Mary Sunshine."

Damian cocked his head to the side, peered out of eyes that were puffy and gritty from lack of sleep, and his mouth lifted in an automatic smile.

"Martha, you're a sight for sore eyes." He crossed the wide hallway in four long strides and caught the diminutive woman in a hug that had her laughing and gasping for breath.

"Put me down, you big gorilla!" Martha swatted ineffectually at his shoulders, blue eyes warm and fond, and Damian laughed, setting her on her feet. She had to crane her neck to look up at him, and, when she did, a frown drew her eyebrows together.

"*Tired eyes* is more like it. You look fit to drop, sweetie."

Damian's heart warmed at her overt concern. Martha Martin had been the family's cook since Damian was a child, and had been a very dear friend to his mother. Growing up, Damian had spent a lot of time in the company of the two women, and had come to think of Martha as something of a surrogate mother.

"Don't worry, Ma, I'm just a bit tired." He looked around him, then added in a conspiratorial tone, "I've been spending most of my time at the office so Naomi can't drag me into helping with the plans for her big shindig. Nothing wrong with me that a cup of strong coffee and some scrambled eggs won't fix." He winked and gave her his sweetest smile.

Martha sighed. "Party, party, party, that's all I've heard for weeks. I tell you, I'll be glad when the whole thing is over."

"You and me both, Ma, you and me both. They in there?" He tilted his head towards the nearest door.

Patting his arm, Martha nodded. "You go on through, love, I'll bring you some breakfast. Would you like some toast with your eggs?"

"Thanks, Ma." Damian smiled, but it twisted into another yawn as he opened the door to the morning room and entered.

Sunshine filled the room, casting a warm glow, and a soft breeze drifted in through the open French windows. Later in the summer they would probably take breakfast on the flagstone terrace outside, but this early in June it was still a little too cool to be completely comfortable at that hour.

"It's about time you surfaced." The voice came from behind a newspaper, but, even though his father couldn't see him, Damian smiled.

"Good morning to you, too, Pa." He enjoyed his father's flinch at the use of the nickname and seated himself at the table, opposite his stepmother, with his father at his rightful place at the head of the table. "Morning, Naomi."

Naomi smiled distractedly, immediately turning her attention to the pile of catalogues, brochures and paperwork beside her, making notes with a silver Montblanc pen that he suspected was from his mother's desk. Damian looked away quickly. His mother had been gone for ten years now, and Naomi—still in her mid-forties—had been married to his father for four of those years, but every now and then it still made something twist in Damian's gut to see another woman sitting in her chair. Using her pen.

"You're looking very casual today; did I miss a memo?" his father asked with an arched eyebrow, lowering his newspaper and reaching for the crystal bowl holding the marmalade. At sixty, Grayson was still a handsome man. Hair grey now, where it had once been the same blond as Damian's, he worked hard at keeping trim and wore his Savile Row suits with easy grace and elegance.

Damian slouched in his chair and rubbed a hand over his face. "I'm taking today off; Alex is coming up for the weekend." He didn't miss the slight deepening of his father's frown.

"That's nice," Naomi said, attention still on her notes. "We haven't seen him for ages. Where has he been, anyway?"

"Alex and a group of other doctors and nurses went out to Africa with an aid agency. He spent two years helping to set up a clinic in a small village." Damian swallowed a sigh. He knew he had told his stepmother this at least twice before, but she didn't seem to take in anything that didn't impact directly on her own life.

"Well, that's lovely. Is he going to be here for the party?" She tucked a lock of expertly coloured blonde hair behind her ear, turned to a stack of post and started opening the envelopes with a knife. Would she even notice if he didn't answer her?

"Yes, as I said, he's going to be here for the weekend." He smiled, pleasure at the thought of seeing his best friend again blooming warmly in his chest.

Martha came in then and set a heaped plate of scrambled eggs and toast in front of Damian, and coffee in a big earthenware mug that clashed horribly with the delicate china the others were drinking from. Damian smiled his thanks and Martha squeezed his shoulder lightly before leaving without a word.

"You're taking time off? Just like that?" Grayson asked, blue-grey eyes intent on his son. "You didn't consider…running this past me?"

You mean ask your permission? Damn it, he was a director at Stanhope Developments, not a bloody secretary. Damian bristled, but he held his tongue. He was in too good a mood this morning to spoil it by getting into a fight with his father. "There's nothing that needs my immediate attention, and my assistant can handle anything that comes in."

He could feel Grayson glaring at him, but Damian refused to back down. He met his father's eyes unflinchingly, a half smile curling one side of his mouth.

"Fine," Grayson bit out, clearly reluctant. Pushing his breakfast plate aside, he stood and picked up his newspaper, tucking it under his arm like a Sergeant Major with his pace stick, his back as ramrod straight as that of any military man Damian had ever seen. "Take your time off, but if there's an emergency I *will* be calling you."

Damian nodded, his mouth occupied with chewing his toast. He wondered what exactly constituted an emergency in his father's head? Earthquake? Hurricane? Running out of paperclips?

Muttering something under his breath, Grayson nodded briefly to Naomi and spared Damian one last *look* before leaving.

"Well, I have things to do. You have fun with your friend, dear." Naomi got to her feet, smoothed her hands over the skirt of her Dior suit and gathered up her things. Before she even reached the door she was punching a number into her phone.

Shortly after she'd left the morning room, Damian heard the door to the library open and close softly, and he felt a twinge in the region of his heart. His mother had spent most of her time during her last months holed up in the library with her beloved books, increasingly removed from life, as if she could find something there that was lacking in the world around her.

Damian could understand that. The feeling that there was something missing occasionally threatened to overwhelm him. Perhaps that was why he had married Shannon? She had been so vibrant, the life and soul of the party. Maybe he had thought that her extrovert personality would be big enough to fill the hollow place inside him?

Damian sighed and laid his fork down on his plate, appetite fading fast. It wasn't until after he'd put the ring on her finger that he'd discovered Shannon was just trying to fill her own hollow place with designer clothes, celebrity-infested nightclubs and whatever diet, beauty regimen or exercise programme *Vogue* happened to be promoting that month. It didn't take him long to realise that Shannon's hand was in his wallet more often than it was in his trousers, and the fact that he didn't particularly care was a pretty big indicator that they weren't going to be seeing any milestone anniversaries together.

A decent financial settlement had ensured her agreement to a quickie divorce, leaving Damian staring down the barrel of a rapidly approaching thirty-fifth birthday with three ex-wives, a diminished bank balance and a general sense of dissatisfaction with life that sat in his chest like a jagged stone.

"Not hungry?" Martha's soft enquiry made Damian jump, his elbow hitting his fork and sending it clattering off his plate onto the table.

"Damn, Martha, you're like a ninja!" He laughed a little breathlessly as his pulse settled back into a more comfortable rate.

"It's what I do in my spare time." Martha pointed at his plate. "Something wrong with your food?"

Damian looked at his half-eaten breakfast and shook his head. "You know you're the best cook in the county, woman. Stop fishing for compliments."

"Then why are you letting it sit there getting cold?" She arched an eyebrow at him in an expression he remembered from his childhood, whenever she had caught him sneaking a biscuit before supper.

He shrugged and gave her an apologetic smile. "Sorry, I was just…thinking."

Martha's face softened. "Deep thoughts by the looks of things."

"I...uh... I suppose I was wallowing more than thinking, really," he admitted, the heat of embarrassment touching his cheeks.

Planting her hands on her hips, Martha squinted at him. "Hmm. Well, you can stop that right now, you hear? Did I hear that Alex was coming to see us?"

Like the flick of a switch, that brought a wide smile to Damian's mouth. Just the mention of his friend felt like the light at the end of the tunnel.

"He should be here some time this afternoon." A knot of almost childlike excitement tightened Damian's stomach at the thought of seeing Alex. Damn, it had been too long.

Martha smiled, warmth and pleasure lighting her grey eyes. "Maybe I'll bake him a cake—coconut?"

"Lemon drizzle," Damian corrected, getting up from the table. "That's his favourite. Oh, and some of those little jam tart thingies. And if you happen to have a steak pie tucked away in the freezer?"

Eyes narrowing slightly, Martha regarded him intently for a moment before nodding. "Okay then, I'll see what I can do."

"Thanks, Ma, you're a star." Damian leaned in and kissed the woman's soft cheek. "I think I'll head down to the stables and take Apollo out for a run. He'll be thinking I've forgotten all about him."

"That sounds like a good idea; you could use a little sun about you after all the time you've spent stuck in that office recently." She looked at his uneaten food again. "And while you're at it, try to work up a bit of an appetite. I won't have you getting sick."

Damian laughed as he watched her leave, still muttering under her breath. He took a moment to swallow the last of his cooling coffee, and then headed upstairs to change, feeling decidedly lighter in spirit than he had in a long while.

Chapter Three

Damian's family was rich. Alex tended to forget this fact until he was faced with the evidence of it whenever he arrived at Garnet House, their estate in Wiltshire. A fortune founded in property and built on the development of world-class holiday resorts afforded the family the kind of lifestyle that was beyond the imagination of most people.

Manoeuvring his car along a lengthy driveway flanked by an avenue of horse chestnuts offering a glimpse of parkland beyond, Alex wondered — not for the first time — what it must have been like for Damian growing up here. There was enough open space to run in, trees to climb and nooks to hide in to satisfy an army of young boys, but Alex had always felt a sense of...loneliness here. Because there *wasn't* an army of young boys; there had just been Damian, with only the occasional nanny as his playmate, and a little sister nearly ten years his junior.

Of course, Damian had been sent away to boarding school when he was just nine, so maybe after being surrounded by hundreds of pre-pubescent boys it was a blessing to come back to the peace and quiet of Garnet House. Alex shook his head with a wry smile. It was another world.

The house came into view then, the honey-coloured stone glowing in the midday sun, light bouncing off the glass of the mullioned bay windows.

"Definitely another world." He drew the car to a halt on the circular forecourt in front of the house, got out and looked up…and up, craning his neck to take in the gabled roofline and the carved stone balustrading over the upper floor windows, hand shielding his eyes from the sunlight.

A noise caught Alex's attention and he lowered his eyes to see one of the double oak front doors open to reveal a rather stern-looking woman in a grey dress and neatly pinned hair almost the same colour. When the woman saw Alex, her mouth turned up in a smile and her blue eyes lit with pleasure, transforming her countenance entirely.

"Well, my goodness, look what the wind blew in."

Alex went to meet her, holding out his hand in greeting. "Hello, Helen, you're looking well."

Laughing, Helen Anderson took Alex's hand between both of hers. "You're almost as bad as Damian with the flattery; I look like a prison warden and you know it."

Alex snickered, but didn't argue. When he was fourteen he'd had to read the Daphne du Maurier novel *Rebecca* in school, and the character of Mrs Danvers had scared the shit out of him. Meeting Mrs Anderson, the Stanhopes' housekeeper, for the first time just five years later had had much the same effect.

"Come on in then." Helen dropped his hand and gestured to the door. "I believe Damian is still down at the stables exercising Apollo, but we can get you settled in your room. Are you hungry after your journey? I'm sure Martha would be more than happy to make you something to eat."

Alex grabbed his bag from the back seat of the car and followed Helen inside. It was a little cooler in the house, and it took Alex's eyes a minute to adjust to the dimmer light.

Nothing about Garnet House had changed since Alex's first visit fifteen years before. The walls were still lined with burnished wood panels, the rugs covering the hardwood floor were the same antique Persian designs, slightly threadbare in parts from generations of wear, and there was still the smell of beeswax and roses in the air.

Helen led the way upstairs and along the first floor hallway, the floorboards creaking under their feet.

"I've put you in your usual room, so you know where everything is."

The bedroom was decorated in shades of cream and blue with heavy, royal blue curtains at the big bay window, pulled back to show off the stunning view of the formal gardens at the back of the house.

Alex placed his bag on the end of the bed and walked over to the window.

"Thank you, Helen. Oh my, I always forget how very beautiful this view is." His voice trailed off as his gaze moved over the copse of trees that concealed the tennis court and beyond that the stable yard.

"Indeed it is. Would you like me to ask Martha to make you some lunch?" Alex looked over his shoulder to see Helen standing in the doorway.

He smiled and shook his head before turning back to the window. "No, thanks. I think I'll take a walk down to the stables and meet Damian."

The door closed quietly behind Helen as she left, and Alex stood at the window for another few minutes before moving to the bed, where he opened his bag and withdrew a camera. Hooking the strap around his neck, he settled the camera comfortably against his chest and headed out.

The sun was high in the clear blue sky as Alex walked along the narrow paths that dissected the flower beds. He stopped occasionally and lifted the camera, snapping shots of irises and lavender, a wisteria covered pergola and the stunning array of colours in the rose garden. The camera—a pretty expensive Pentax digital SLR—was identical to the one Alex had taken out to Africa with him. He was never getting that one back. He'd taken thousands of photographs out there, moments of beauty and happiness that, if he were able to look at them now, might go some way to tempering the darkness of those last few days.

Following a gravel-covered path through a grove of cypress firs with a stone folly at the centre, it was a good ten-minute walk to the stable yard. The earthy smell in the air strengthened as he got closer, until he finally turned a corner and the stables came into view. He paused for a moment and took a few pictures. As he did so, an elderly man wandered into his shot. Alex lowered the camera and smiled.

Harry Grace, the head groom, raised an arm in greeting as Alex came towards him. Somewhere in his mid-seventies, Harry was a weather-worn man with untamed wiry grey hair and a ruddy complexion.

"Alex, I heard talk of you visiting. Good to see you again." Harry's voice was as rough as the rest of him, but there was a distinctly youthful glint in his sharp blue eyes.

After two years of manual labour out in Africa, Alex's hands were tougher and more callused than they had ever been, but, next to the old groom's hands, Alex's were baby soft. Harry also had a grip that made Alex wince inwardly.

"It's good to be back, Harry. How are you?"

"Fighting fit, lad, fighting fit." Harry jerked a thumb over his shoulder. "Damian's still out with Apollo; he should be back soon."

"Thanks, Harry. I'll just take a wander around, if that's okay?" Alex indicated the camera around his neck.

"Have at it. If you want a cup of tea there's always a brew going in the tack room." With a small wave, Harry went back to his work.

Alex decided not to take him up on the tea. He'd experienced Harry's tea before — in a pinch it could be used to tarmac a road.

There were ten loose boxes in the stable block, but only four of them were currently occupied. Alex clicked off some shots of the horses, smiling at the range of emotions the animals threw his way — everything from twitching excitement to curiosity to outright disdain. He petted the long nose of the youngest-looking horse, laughing when it snuffled into his hand, clearly looking for a treat.

The unmistakeable sound of horse's hooves caught Alex's attention, and he turned to see Damian leading Apollo, his palomino, into the yard.

At the sight of his friend, tall, broad and glowing with perspiration from his ride, his thick, dark blond hair blown by the breeze, and twin spots of colour touching his cheeks, something twisted and tightened low in Alex's belly. It was a familiar sensation that he'd experienced for the first time on their initial meeting at university, aged nineteen, and every time since. But Alex had had fifteen years of practice at quickly suppressing the feeling, so the switch that flicked from *desire* to *friend* was now automatic.

"Well, if it isn't the African Queen!" A wide grin split Damian's face and mischief sparkled in his blue eyes.

Alex snickered. "Fuck you, Little Lord Fauntleroy."

When they'd closed the distance between them, Damian hauled him into a one-armed hug, squashing him between his broad chest and Apollo's muscled neck. Laughing, Alex gasped for breath, smelling sweat and horses and just a hint of soap.

"Jesus, you reek!" Alex pushed him away, wrinkling his nose in distaste, but still laughing.

"I smell like man," Damian declared, squaring his shoulders and puffing out his chest.

"You smell like horse's arse." Alex punched him on the arm and dodged the smack Damian aimed at his head.

"Better than looking like one." Damian's grin held the smug gleam of victory.

Alex feigned an insulted expression. "Hey! I'm fucking beautiful, I am."

"You've been listening to your mother again, haven't you?" Damian shook his head sadly. "How many times do I have to tell you mother's opinions don't count? Even the Elephant Man's mother thought he was pretty."

Alex slapped him on the shoulder and they fell easily into step. At Apollo's box, Alex stood to the side and watched Damian take care of his horse. He couldn't resist taking a few photographs as Damian spoke in gentle tones to the big animal while he brushed him down. It was soothing to watch, and, after the unremitting din of his parents' house, the peace and quiet was a blessed relief.

Through the viewfinder of the camera, Alex watched the shift of Damian's muscles under his skin, the beads of sweat that rolled from the hair at the nape of his neck to be absorbed by his T-shirt. Heat unfurled in Alex and his pulse kicked up a notch. He lowered the camera and closed his eyes, taking a deep breath in an attempt to restore his sense of calm. *Not good, Jennings, not good at all.*

"You okay?" Alex opened his eyes at the sound of Damian's voice, and found his friend watching him with concern in his eyes.

Giving himself a mental shake and raising an eyebrow, Alex smiled. "I'm starving, so if you've quite finished whispering sweet nothings in your boy's ear…"

Damian replied with a smirk and a hand gesture unfit for mixed company.

They walked back up to the house, but instead of going around to the front door they headed for the rear of the building, and the entrance to the kitchen. The top half of the Dutch door had been left open, so Damian leaned on the bottom half and stuck his head in.

"Hey, Ma, I'm home and I brought you a present."

"Stop right where you are, Damian Stanhope. I've just cleaned my floor, and if you've been down at that smelly stable block…" Martha was across the kitchen and beside them faster than Alex would have thought possible, wielding a wooden spoon threateningly. But when she looked over Damian's shoulder her eyes widened, and the pleasure that lit them warmed Alex.

Opening the door and shoving Damian aside rather unceremoniously, Martha stuck the spoon in the pocket of her apron, stepped forwards and cupped Alex's face between her hands. "Let me look at you; did you take care of yourself out there? Did you eat properly?"

Damian groaned. "Oh God, Ma, you're not going to ask him about his bowel movements, are you? Because, if you are, I'm leaving now."

"I would threaten to slap you silly, boy, but nature got there before me." Martha scowled in Damian's direction, but Alex could see the fondness in her eyes.

"I'm fine, Martha." Alex smiled and cocked his head to the side. "Maybe a little hungry?"

Martha opened the door and ushered them in. "Well, I just happen to have a lemon drizzle cake with your name on it — Damian Stanhope, take your boots off and wash your hands before you even think about sitting at my table."

While Martha disappeared into the pantry and Alex took a seat, Damian kicked off his boots and headed for the sink, mumbling under his breath about the unfairness of it all.

The kitchen was a cavernous room, built at a time when space was needed to accommodate the multitude of staff required to cater for grand balls and house parties. It was dominated by a massive, scarred pine table and an Aga that was terrifying in its complexity to a man like Alex, whose culinary expertise extended to the microwave and the speed dial button on the phone he'd programmed with the number of his favourite pizza place.

Alex let his eyes travel around the room until it came to rest on Damian at the big Belfast sink under the window. He had taken off his T-shirt and was up to his elbows in soapy water, the smooth skin of his back stretched over tight muscle, jeans riding low on narrow hips and hugging his backside *just right*.

Fuck. Tearing his gaze away from his friend, Alex shifted in his chair as his cock stirred, and his pulse raced uncomfortably. Clearly, his time away had left him a little less practiced at controlling himself than he used to be. He was going to have to be a bit more vigilant if he didn't want the shit to hit the fan.

Chapter Four

Damian pushed his empty plate aside and slouched in his chair at the big kitchen table, coffee mug cradled in his hands. He watched, a smile curving his lips, as Alex laid siege to Martha's home-baked lemon drizzle cake. Always on the lean side, he was thinner than he'd been the last time Damian had seen him — *damn*, had it really been *two years*? His cheekbones seemed sharper, his blue-green eyes bigger in his face, and his muscles more sinewy. But his skin was deeply tanned, practically radiating good health. His hair, too, usually the colour of sable, was showing the effects of long-term exposure to the sun, bleached several shades lighter in places. Damian had seen people pay a small fortune to hairdressers in an attempt to achieve that look.

"So, are you home for good or what?"

Alex's fork halted halfway to his mouth and his eyes widened before they seemed to...cloud over, some emotion flashing through them too quickly to be identified. He shrugged — a tight hitch of his shoulders. "Uh, I'm not really sure yet."

Damian felt his own eyebrows pull together in a frown as he watched Alex return to eating his cake with all the gusto of a starving man, but it was clearly now more of a delaying tactic than genuine enjoyment. Damian knew Alex's face as well as he knew his own, and he recognised the lines of tension that suddenly appeared at the corners of his friend's eyes. Oh yes, there was definitely a story there.

It took a simple tilt of the head for Damian to let Alex know he wasn't going to let it go at that; Alex knew him equally well.

With a small sigh, Alex cast a glance in Martha's direction, and Damian nodded. Whatever Alex had to say, he didn't want to say it in front of Martha. Damian could wait.

Shaking off his concerns for the moment, Damian leant forward, set down his mug and rested his elbows on the edge of the table. "Did you bring me something?" he asked, grinning.

Alex snorted, coughed and took a gulp of coffee to wash down the cake on which he was obviously in danger of choking. Martha tut-tutted and pinched Damian's ear—he would deny to his dying day that he'd squealed like a little girl.

"You're a mercenary little sod, Damian Stanhope. It's enough that Alex came back to us safe and in one piece." She smiled sweetly at Alex and poured more coffee into his mug.

Damian rubbed his ear. "Come on, Ma, I can't tell him that, he'll think... I *like* him or something. Oh! And little?" He crooked an eyebrow significantly.

"I do *not* want to know," Martha stated, throwing her hands up to cover her ears.

Damian laughed and turned his attention back to Alex, eyebrow still arched.

"You are a child. A six-foot-two, seventy-two kilogram, over-educated *child*," Alex said, his face as expressionless as his voice was bland.

"Seventy kilogram. Did you bring me something?" He tried his most charming smile — it worked on most women; why not a gay man?

Alex rolled his eyes and pushed away from the table. "I think you've probably had enough sugar, and I'm sure Martha's had enough of you. Martha, it's lovely to see you again, and the cake was almost as delicious as you." With a grin Alex went to the elderly woman and caught her up in a bear hug.

"I'm very happy you're home, love," she said, rubbing a hand over his back.

Damian shook his head, doing his best to feign disgust, even as his smile refused to be concealed. "Talk about sugar! That was so sweet I may have to make an appointment with my dentist."

"You might, at that," Martha retorted, brandishing a tiny, clenched fist at him, her blue eyes glittering with humour.

"Come on, mate, you wouldn't last a single round against Martha." Alex took Damian's arm and tugged him towards the door. His hand was warm, his grip strong on Damian's forearm, and Damian felt an odd little...tingle run the length of the limb, the sensation lingering a moment even after Alex had broken contact.

Damian frowned, puzzled. How strange.

"I should have a shower; I'm starting to stink up the place," Damian said when they pushed through the door that separated the long corridor leading to the kitchen and utility rooms from the main hallway.

"You're just noticing this now?" Alex grinned widely, bumping Damian's shoulder with his own.

Damian bumped back. "Fuck you, Jennings. I can't believe I actually missed you." There was no heat, only humour in his voice.

He'd taken several steps before he realised Alex was no longer beside him. Stopping, Damian turned to find Alex standing a few feet away, his head tilted slightly to the side, smiling softly.

"You missed me?" he asked.

Something curled tight in Damian's stomach, and when he laughed it felt a little hollow, breathless. He had to fight the urge to cross his arms over his chest. "Well, of course I did, you bloody fool. You're my best friend."

Alex was silent for a long moment, then his smile widened and the warmth in his eyes deepened. He started moving again, heading towards the curved staircase. As he passed Damian he patted him on the stomach. "It's always nice to hear. Now go and shower then come and get me. I'll be in my room."

At the light touch, Damian sucked in his already flat stomach, and there it was again, that...*tingle*, this time accompanied by a rush of heat that started at his toes and chased the blood through his veins until he felt like he had a fever, felt like his skin was too tight for his body. He drew in a deep, shaky breath, and turned to see Alex climbing the stairs, two at a time, his movements athletic and elegant.

It was surprisingly difficult for Damian to drag his eyes away, and, when he finally moved, his legs felt stiff and heavy. He was quite a way behind Alex, so by the time he got to the next floor Alex had already disappeared into his bedroom. Damian entered his own bedroom, four doors down from Alex's, with the same splendid view of the formal gardens.

He undressed distractedly, letting his dirty clothes fall on the floor to be collected and put into the hamper later. Helen had drummed into him a long time ago that she was a housekeeper, not a nanny, and if he wanted his clothes cleaned then he could damn well pick up after himself like the adult he supposedly was.

Naked, he went to the adjoining bathroom and turned on the shower. When the water reached the temperature he wanted—cooler than usual, but he was suddenly so damn *warm*—he stepped in and shoved his head under the showerhead. A shiver ran through him when the water touched his skin, but it quickly banished the rather uncomfortable heat from his blood. He washed with the citrus-scented soap he preferred and shampooed his hair. The water cascaded over his shoulders and down his body as he scrubbed at his scalp, and he was soon feeling considerably more like himself, whatever had come over him washing away with the soap down the drain.

When he'd finished washing his hair he turned and ducked under the deluge again, bracing one hand against the tiles, and running the other slowly down his chest, over the ridges of his stomach and down to the tangle of blond pubic hair, darkened by the water. He started using the foam slipping down his body to wash his genitals, but at the first touch of his fingers his cock began to harden, and with just a couple of strokes he was rigid and aching. He gasped and the fingers resting on the tile curled into a fist.

He often got hard in the shower, and when he didn't have company he was used to taking care of matters for himself, but he couldn't recall ever getting this stiff this fast—with or without company. His cock pulsed in his hand, the head almost painfully sensitive when he ran his thumb over it. He could already feel the prickle of oncoming orgasm at the base of his spine; the tightening of his sac. Sucking his lower lip between his teeth, he tightened his hand around his straining flesh and his hips jerked as he fucked his hand. God that felt good!

Pre-cum was leaking profusely from the slit now, and the muscles in his thighs and lower belly were starting to quiver. Damian picked up the pace, breath coming in shallow pants before stuttering to a halt altogether when an explosive orgasm overtook him. His seed spurted hot and fast, hitting the tiles and coating his hand.

He leaned against the shower wall for long moments afterwards, letting the water wash him and the tiles clean again while he regained his composure and remembered how to breathe.

When he finally turned off the water and got out of the shower his muscles felt loose and relaxed. He dried off with languid movements and dressed in a fresh polo shirt and jeans. He slipped his bare feet into a well-worn pair of deck shoes and left the room, heading for Alex's room with a smile he was sure was smug and probably screamed of how pleasant his shower had been.

Knocking once on the door as a courtesy, Damian entered the room and his eyes were immediately drawn to his friend, stretched out on the bed, eyes closed, snoring lightly. Laughing softly, he allowed his gaze to linger a moment, to appreciate the presence of his friend before he turned away and looked around the room.

Alex clearly hadn't had time to unpack yet—his bag was sitting open on the padded window seat—but he had taken out his laptop and it was sitting on the escritoire opposite the bed, connected up to the camera. Damian wandered over and sat in the spindle-backed chair at the desk, and was soon flipping through the photographs Alex had taken that afternoon. He was surprised and impressed by how professional they looked, and laughed again when he came to the pictures of himself with Apollo, the horse nuzzling into him, clearly in search of a treat.

A soft sound from the direction of the bed caught Damian's attention. When he turned a frown immediately creased his brow.

Alex was moving his head from side to side on the pillow, eyes moving rapidly behind his lids, hands clenched into tight fists at his sides. Damian got to his feet and went to the side of the bed. He laid a gentle hand on Alex's shoulder, but it failed to rouse his friend so he shook him a little. Alex's eyes flew open, but continued to move from side to side, unfocused.

"Alex, are you all right?" Damian kept his voice low, not wanting to startle the man.

Without warning, Alex reared up, and the look in his eyes was nothing short of terrified. His whole body was shaking, his breathing shallow and uneven, and there was a film of sweat on his forehead.

Something sharp lodged in Damian's chest, and without hesitation he sat on the edge of the bed and pulled Alex into his arms. Damian held on tightly, one hand spread across Alex's back, the other cupping the back of his head. Alex continued to tremble in his arms. Damian had never felt so ineffectual in his life.

Chapter Five

Alex sat on the steps of the small red-brick building at the side of the tennis court, enjoying the late afternoon sun and the gentle breeze rustling through the high hedge bordering the area. He was grateful to Damian for suggesting they get out of the house for a while. Waking from one of those dreams always left him feeling trapped and claustrophobic. The residual memory of the dream made him shudder, and he had no wish to recount it, but he knew he had to give Damian an explanation.

A different kind of shiver ran through him at the thought of his friend. In spite of the fear and panic that had remained when he'd woken from the dream, Alex couldn't help thinking about how it had felt to be wrapped in Damian's arms. They had hugged before, of course, the embrace of friends greeting each other, congratulatory hugs or a promise to see each other again soon. But this had been no manly slap on the back. Damian had *held* him, smoothed his hand over Alex's back, tangled his fingers in Alex's hair. It had been intended to comfort, and it had, but it had also tapped into the deeply buried ache in Alex that yearned to be more to Damian than a friend.

Alex scrubbed a hand through his hair and pulled his knees closer to conceal the stirring of his cock in his jeans. He felt a stab of shame that his body should take an act of friendship at its purest and turn it into something base. He couldn't quite meet Damian's eyes when he came out of the small pavillion carrying two bottles of beer.

"Thanks," Alex said, taking the proffered bottle and leaning back against one of the posts supporting the portico while Damian settled into a wicker chair with his own drink. Damian was obviously trying to look nonchalant, but Alex could read the concern in the lines around his friend's eyes, and in the tight set of his jaw.

Lowering his eyes to the bottle in his hand, Alex trailed a finger through the condensation beading on the surface and took a gulp to moisten his suddenly dry throat. "It wasn't my choice to leave Africa," he started, surprised when his voice came out strong and even. He certainly didn't feel strong *or* even.

Damian didn't make any kind of response, but Alex could feel the weight of his gaze on him, offering silent encouragement.

Ignoring the clench of anxiety in his stomach, Alex set his bottle down beside him and clasped his hands together between his drawn up knees. "We did a lot of good work out there. People from the villages around the clinic were coming to us to be treated for everything from cholera to malaria to measles, and we administered vaccines to the people who hadn't yet been struck down. We set up an antiretroviral programme for those with HIV and AIDS, and carried out more surgical procedures than I can count. We even helped install water purification systems. It was exhausting work, but..."

"Fulfilling?" Damian supplied quietly.

Alex sighed raggedly as emotion rose and clogged his throat. "God, yes. Do you have any idea how it feels to restore the sight of a young mother with one simple operation, and watch as she sees her baby for the first time?"

"I can't begin to imagine," Damian replied. He was leaning forwards now, elbows resting on his knees, beer bottle dangling between his fingers.

"There were some people we couldn't help, though, and that just never gets easier." Alex took another drink and swallowed with some difficulty before continuing. "There was a lot of conflict in the region between two warring militia factions, and we were often called upon to help wounded soldiers, most of them barely out of adolescence. One faction took control of the area we were operating in, and they made it clear that we were not to treat anyone from the opposing faction. But we were doctors, for fuck's sake, what were we supposed to do when a ten-year-old boy was brought in with his leg blown off and bleeding out in front of us? They called him a *soldier*. A ten-year-old boy!" He was on his feet and looking out over the tennis court before he even realised he was moving. He jumped when he felt the light touch of a hand on his back, and turned his head to see Damian standing beside him.

"Go on," Damian encouraged with a small nod.

Alex allowed himself to lean back into the reassuring touch. "We helped the boy, of course; stopped the bleeding and treated him for an infection. He was of no use as a soldier any more, and had no family to take care of him, so a woman in one of the villages took him in. She came rushing into the clinic one day soon after, told us that the boy's enemies had taken him." Alex pulled away and spun around to face Damian. "In what kind of world does a child have enemies?"

"What happened to him?" Dread was clear in Damian's voice, and his blue eyes were narrowed, as if bracing himself.

"His body was found dumped by the roadside two days later. He was shot in the head." Grief and regret squeezed Alex's chest, making it hard to breathe.

"Jesus." Damian slumped back against the post opposite, face ashen, and for the first time in his life Alex understood the phrase *he went pale under his tan*. "That's not everything, is it?"

After a pause, Alex shook his head. "When they found out we'd given help to the enemy, the local militia came to the clinic. They rounded up all the aid workers at gunpoint, herded us onto an open-top truck and drove us out of the village for the last time. For the next two days we were driven through searing heat during the day and freezing cold at night, without a drop of food or water, most of us just wearing the T-shirts we'd been taken in. It wasn't pleasant, but it was just a couple of days, right? I mean, the people we were trying to help had been through a hell of a lot more for a hell of a lot longer."

"But?" Damian asked, almost as if he was afraid to ask, to hear.

Alex's throat felt like it was closing up on him, reluctant to speak the words. He had to turn away from Damian, unable to bear the fear he could see in his friend's eyes when he himself was almost consumed by the emotion. "The soldiers who rode in the truck with us took great pleasure in taunting us.

They were armed with AK-47s, and would point them at us, make us choose if we wanted to lose a leg or a hand. There was one…he had a revolver, an old-looking thing. He…" Alex had to stop, ran a hand over his face and dragged it through his hair again. "He would put one bullet in the gun, pick one of us, aim at our heads and…and pull the trigger. He thought it was hilarious. I've never been so fucking scared in my life. Every time he held that gun in front of my face and pulled the trigger, I thought my heart was going to stop. When they dumped us out of the truck at the border I was sure we were going to be killed. I couldn't believe it when they just drove away and left us there."

"Christ almighty, Alex. I don't… I can't…" Damian's voice hitched and he moved closer, laid a trembling hand on the back of Alex's neck.

Alex turned back to Damian and felt a sudden need to reassure him. Ignoring the turmoil roiling in his own chest, he lifted a hand and curled it around Damian's wrist. "It's okay. *I'm* okay. Look at me." He gave Damian's wrist a little shake.

"I never imagined… It—it's so bloody horrifying. What if…?"

"No!" Alex interrupted sharply, thinking now only of Damian. "No what-ifs. I'm here; it's over." It was easier to smile than Alex would have believed just moments ago.

Damian drew himself up to his full height then—just an inch taller than Alex—and his face took on a serious, determined set. "You're not going back," he stated sharply.

Unexpected laughter burst from Alex. Shit! Only Damian could make him laugh when just seconds before he'd been locked in the memory of his darkest moment. "Is that right?"

"I won't allow it," Damian reaffirmed, nodding for emphasis. "My God, man, when I think about what might have happened to you…"

"Don't think about it, Damian, please." Alex tightened his grip on Damian's wrist imploringly. "I'm safe. I'm *safe*. And as for going back, well, that's out of my hands. When we finally managed to get in touch with the agency, they got us out of there quick smart; and pulled out all of their workers from the surrounding area. They're not willing to send anyone back in until they can be assured of their workers' safety."

"Well, all right then. Good. That's good." Damian's expression turned sheepish then, and he lowered his eyes momentarily, before meeting Alex's gaze again. "And that may be the most selfish thing I've ever said. What about the clinic? You must be concerned for all the people you had to leave behind."

Something twisted in Alex's chest when he thought of all the wonderful people who had become a part of his everyday life; of perhaps never seeing them again. "The clinic is still there, and we trained some of the locals in basic medical care. I can only hope that's enough until the agency can get people back out there. On a personal level, it… Well, I believe the term is *it sucks!*" His laughter was hollow, humourless, but Damian smiled anyway, and Alex felt something loosen inside him. "Well, I think that's enough of this soul-searching nonsense for one day, don't you? How about another beer and you can tell me what's happening in the world of resort development?"

Damian rolled his eyes. "God, no! I've had my fill of work recently. How about I see if there's a bottle of the good stuff in there and we have a re-match?" He gestured in the direction of the ball machine at the end of the court.

Laughter exploded from Alex as he recalled the night, a few years ago when they had sloped out of a dinner party up at the house, liberating a bottle of twenty-year-old single malt on the way, and had come down here. He didn't remember whose idea the drinking game had been — the object to hit every ball the machine issued, and take a shot of whisky for every miss — only that they'd both ended up too incapacitated to even make it back to the house, and had woken the next morning, sprawled on the floor of the pavillion, cold and very hung over. "Do you even remember who won the first round?"

"No fucking idea." Damian snickered. "All the more reason to settle the point. No?"

In the end, finding nothing harder in the bar, they settled for a couple more beers, and sat together on the porch, talking about nothing more traumatising than the latest rugby scores, and Alex soon found himself relaxing, his anxieties sloughing off like dead skin.

Chapter Six

Damian felt unsettled. His stomach churned like he'd had a bad takeaway, and his skin prickled with agitation. He kept up his end of the conversation as he walked back to the house with Alex, but a little voice in his head kept up a determined litany of *what if, what if, what if,* tormenting him with mental images of his best friend with a gun pressed to his head, wounded, bleeding... He found himself walking closer to Alex than he normally would, touching him more — a hand on the shoulder, a pat on the back — with an irresistible need to reassure himself that everything was all right. Alex was here. Alex was safe.

Anything else was simply unbearable to even think about. *What if, what if, what if,* the voice continued to badger him, until Damian wanted to scream *shut up, just shut the fuck up!* Instead, he tucked his hands into his pockets, fists clenched tightly. He couldn't—wouldn't—let Alex see the effect his ordeal was having on him; the man clearly had enough to cope with in dealing with his own emotions in the aftermath.

A part of Damian wondered at his own reaction to what Alex had told him. Alex was the best friend he'd ever had, yes, but this knife to the gut feeling Damian couldn't seem to shake off rang an alarm bell that he instinctively shied away from examining too closely.

"What on earth?" Alex stopped walking when they turned the corner to the side of the house.

Halting beside his friend, Damian followed the direction of Alex's confused gaze to the marquee erected on the lawn, and turned back to him, frowning his own puzzlement. "Something wrong?"

Eyes narrowed, Alex brought his attention to Damian. "When you said there was going to be 'a bit of a bash', exactly what did you mean?"

"A bash, you know, a party," Damian explained, baffled.

"I know what a bash is, you arse," Alex sighed. "But I was expecting a dinner party, maybe ten or twelve people, twenty max. It looks like you're getting set up for a royal wedding here."

Damian snorted. "Oh no, it's much more important than that. It's Pa's sixtieth birthday."

Smacking Damian none too gently on the arm, Alex scowled darkly. "It's bad enough that you invited me to what is clearly going to be a black tie affair without telling me—thus, not giving me a chance to pack an actual black fucking tie. But you're telling me now that this is for your father's birthday? *Now*, when I have no way of getting the guest of honour a damn present!" He smacked Damian's arm again, and Damian stumbled back, grinning.

"Oh, calm down, princess," Damian said, walking backwards, making sure to keep some distance between them. "You can borrow something of mine to wear; I'm sure Helen will be happy to carry out any emergency alterations, and I've got the present covered."

Alex continued to glare for a moment, but Damian saw the annoyance leech out of his blue-green eyes, replaced by reluctant humour. "You're still an arse." Alex lurched forward then, and, seeing the intent in his friend's expression, Damian yelped, spun on his heel and took off, happy to be back on familiar ground with Alex.

Laughing with a freedom he hadn't felt in a long time, Damian managed to stay two steps ahead of Alex, their feet crunching on the gravel path, skidding around the next corner to the front of the house. Just before they reached the front door, something caught Damian's attention and he stopped dead. Having no warning, Alex slammed right into the back of him.

"What?" Alex asked, slightly winded.

Damian's smile faltered when he suddenly became intensely aware of the weight of Alex's hands on his hips. They were so close that Damian could feel the heat of Alex's breath on his neck, and it caused his own breath to stutter in his chest.

"Damian," Alex moved to stand beside him, but Damian could still feel him pressed along the length of his body. "What is it?"

"Hmm? What?" Damian felt oddly distracted. He looked at Alex, but for some reason that did nothing to help him focus, so he glanced away, and his gaze settled once again on the object that had initially made him stop. Something akin to desperation seized him and he was moving again. "Come on, there's someone I want you to meet." Trusting that Alex would follow, Damian strode towards the front door, trailing his fingers over the gleaming paint job of a dark blue Range Rover when he passed it.

He had to blink a few times to adjust to the dim lighting in the reception hall, but his step never slowed as he followed the sound of voices into the informal drawing room, only ever used by the family.

"Okay, where's my favourite girl?"

Four sets of eyes turned towards the door when Damian opened it. He headed directly for the small gathered group, and his younger sister Romilly at its centre. "There she is," Damian said in a hushed, almost reverent voice as he reached for the little bundle of pink in Romilly's arms.

"I remember a time when I was his favourite girl," Romilly said in a teasing tone, relinquishing her baby daughter to her brother's care.

"And I was your hero until you found your very own Mr Darcy." Damian acknowledged his brother-in-law with a smile and a nod, and snuggled the baby in his arms, loving the way she fit so perfectly. He turned towards Alex and tilted the baby slightly so that his friend could see her properly. "Alex, meet the newest addition to the tribe, Annabelle Stanhope-Darcy. We call her Belle."

Stepping closer, Alex eased aside the pink blanket and looked down at the baby staring back at them with huge blue eyes. He smoothed his little finger over the soft curve of her cheek and she turned into the touch, mouth lifting in a smile.

"She's...wow! She's amazing, and very appropriately named." Alex smiled up at Damian, and Damian felt something shift in his chest. Alex moved away to greet Romilly and Damian's gaze followed him as he hugged Romilly and was introduced to her husband Michael for the first time.

Damian was peripherally aware of Martha and Helen excusing themselves to return to work, but he couldn't seem to drag his eyes away from his friend. Something stirred to life in him, something he felt instinctively he ought to understand, but the emotion, the feeling, the *thought* was like a single leaf caught up in a storm—out of his reach and moving too fast for him to keep up.

"When did you get to be so grown up? I can't believe you got married and had a baby," Alex said to Romilly, his tone a mixture of wonder and amusement.

Romilly laughed, an open, joyful sound. "A lot has changed in two years, hasn't it?"

Her words touched something at the very core of Damian, and he held Belle closer as his hands started to shake.

* * * *

"You're very quiet tonight," Romilly said softly, leaning a little closer to Damian at dinner that evening.

Damian took a sip of wine and attempted a smile. "You know I can never get a word in edgeways when you're around."

"That's never stopped you from trying." There was an edge to Romilly's voice that made Damian shift uncomfortably in his seat. "You've been acting...odd all day. What's going on?"

Before he could stop it, Damian's gaze went to Alex, seated at the other side of the table, politely listening to Naomi talk about her party plans. Alex was wearing a dark jacket over a snowy white shirt that complemented his tan. He'd left the top two buttons undone, and when Damian glimpsed the triangle of skin at the hollow of the man's throat, and the scattering of hair that was just visible, a sensation that was all too recognisable tore through him. *Desire*.

He felt the blood drain from his face, and, when he jerked his gaze away from Alex to meet his sister's, Romilly's eyes widened and her mouth parted on a silent gasp. "I—I think I'll just go and check on Belle. Damian, why don't you come with me?" She got to her feet so quickly that her chair rocked back before resettling, her napkin falling unheeded to the floor.

Feeling as though he had taken a blow to the head, Damian could only nod. He stood and followed Romilly from the room, praying that his legs wouldn't give out on him, and most assuredly *not* glancing in Alex's direction.

The second the dining room door closed behind him, Romilly grabbed Damian's hand and rushed him, unresisting, up the stairs and into his own bedroom, where she closed the door and leant back against it.

"Oh, my God," she whispered, and Damian, coming to a halt in the middle of the room, could hear the underlying thrum of excitement in her voice.

He turned to face her, dragging his hands through his hair. "Rom..." He had no idea what he wanted to say. Jesus, what *could* he say? How could he explain that, after three ex-wives and countless fleeting encounters with the female of the species, he was suddenly tied up in knots over things like Alex's skin and his *smile*, when he didn't understand it himself? He was assailed by the memory of Alex pressed up against him that afternoon, touching him from shoulder to knee, body hard and unyielding. Lust, searing in its intensity, lanced through Damian to pool hotly between his legs. He sucked in a shocked, ragged breath and spun on his heel, turning away from his sister as he ripped off his jacket and tie, tossing them aside with complete disregard for expense or workmanship.

"I can't believe this," Romilly breathed. Damian didn't hear her moving, and he flinched when she rested a hand in the middle of his back. He moved away and slumped onto the padded window seat, resting his elbows on his knees and looking down at his feet. She followed and sat beside him. "*Alex*? Oh, my God, this is…this is… Have you always felt this way? How could I not have seen it; I must have been blind."

He was on his feet again, too agitated to sit still, his movements jerky as he paced the carpet, shaking his head. "No, of course I haven't. He's my best friend, for God's sake, *no!*"

"Then what's changed?" Romilly asked quietly, and he could feel her eyes following him.

Damian was still shaking his head as his long strides ate up the floor, back and forth, back and forth. "Nothing. Everything. *Fuck*, I don't know." His heart was beating a rapid tattoo in his chest, his pulse was racing uncomfortably quickly and he could hear the rush of his own blood in his ears.

"Oh dear!" Romilly was beside him in a split second, guiding him to the foot of the bed where he seemed to crumple, falling bonelessly, missing the bed and ending up on his backside on the floor. Romilly crouched before him, blue eyes filled with concern.

How could I not have seen it? Her words echoed in Damian's ears and he felt dizzy. It was as though the very foundations of his life were shifting and he had nothing to hold on to.

Chapter Seven

Waking early the next morning, Alex dressed in jeans and a clean shirt and made his way quietly down to the kitchen in search of caffeine. The house was still and silent at that hour, but Alex could already hear the crew setting up outside in preparation for that night's party. He shook his head, smiling to himself. He should be annoyed at Damian for not giving him all the information when he'd invited him to the party, but he'd always found Damian's happy-go-lucky approach to life to be somewhat endearing. Besides, the chance to see Damian in a dinner jacket was definitely worth a little inconvenience and potential embarrassment.

It was cooler downstairs, and Alex shivered as he crossed the floor to the door that led to the kitchen. The aroma of coffee drifted to him the second he opened the door, and Alex's smile deepened, grateful that Martha was still an early riser. His footsteps faltered at the sound of voices—Martha's and a man's—and he wondered if perhaps he should turn back, but he continued on when he recognised the male voice. When he entered the kitchen he saw Martha in her customary starched white apron, mixing something in a bowl, while seated at the table, a mug of steaming coffee in front of him, was Jude, Grayson Stanhope's driver.

"I'm not interrupting a lovers' tryst, am I?" Alex asked, taking a seat at the table with his back to the window so that the rays of the early morning sun warmed him. He reached for the coffee pot and filled a mug for himself.

"Not right now, but if you'd come in ten minutes ago." Jude winked lasciviously, and Alex snorted.

"He couldn't handle me; I'm far too much woman for a runt like him," Martha retorted, her smile taking any bite out of the words.

Runt was not a word that came to mind when Alex thought of Jude. In what Alex guessed to be his mid to late thirties, Jude was tall and strong with a straight posture and buzzed haircut that hinted at a military background. The man laughed, and it softened his face. Alex wouldn't go so far as to describe Jude as handsome, but he was attractive in a tough, austere way.

"You're probably right, Martha," Jude said, grinning at Alex. "A fragile little flower like me? You'd snap me in two."

"Just you remember that." She pointed the whisk threateningly at Jude before turning away to add something to the bowl.

Jude stirred his coffee absently, shaking his head in amusement. "I heard you were back; how was Africa?" he asked, turning his attention to Alex.

A familiar sinking feeling settled in Alex's stomach, but he determinedly ignored it. He was no more a fragile flower than Jude, and he refused to act like one.

"It was good, thanks. Hotter than hell, of course, but you know how it is." Alex had no idea if Jude knew how it was or not, but he wasn't surprised when the man nodded.

"I certainly do. Sugar?" Jude pushed the bowl across the table, and smiled when Alex shook his head. "Sweet enough already?"

Alex coughed around the mouthful of coffee he'd just taken, and regarded Jude with wide eyes. There was a little twinkle in Jude's green eyes that was more than just amusement. If Alex believed in such a thing as gaydar, his would be going off like Big Ben at midday.

"Am I interrupting?"

Alex started at the sound of Damian's voice and turned to find his friend standing in the kitchen doorway. Laughter bubbled up in Alex's throat, and it was on the tip of his tongue to reply to the question as Jude had replied to his own similar enquiry, but one look at Damian's face told Alex that his friend was in no mood for levity. "You look like the morning after the night before. Come and have some coffee." Alex reached for the pot and another mug, but Damian lingered in the doorway.

"Actually, I won't. I just came to get some apples to take down to the stables." Damian's gaze flicked between Alex and Jude before moving to Martha.

Martha set her bowl down on the table and went to the pantry, returning a few seconds later with a bag of green apples. "You don't look like you should be riding today, love. Are you feeling okay?"

"I'm fine, Ma. It's just like Alex said, I had a little too much to drink last night; my own fault." Damian shrugged and smiled, but it was a pale facsimile of his usual smile.

Alex suppressed a laugh. Damian and Romilly had been huddled together whispering most of the previous night, both at the dinner table and afterwards in the drawing room. Alex guessed they must have continued on long into the night, putting away some of Grayson's finest wine in the process.

"Well, I'm sure the fresh air will do you good," Martha said, returning to her breakfast preparations.

Damian passed the bag of apples from one hand to the other and turned to Alex. "I put my spare dinner jacket and tie in your room. If you need a shirt, just let me know."

Momentary confusion pulled Alex's eyebrows together. Was he imagining the way Damian seemed to be having trouble meeting his eyes? But that made no sense. "That's great, thanks."

"No problem. I'll see you later. Jude." With a brief nod to the driver, Damian turned and left the kitchen through the back door.

"There goes a man who's suffering," Jude said, laughing softly.

Alex nodded, eyes still on the back door. Something didn't *feel* right, but he couldn't quite put his finger on it.

* * * *

"I'm so glad Naomi decided to go with a subtle theme," Romilly said quietly, her voice fairly dripping with sarcasm.

Standing beside her at the entrance to the marquee, Alex supressed a laugh as he looked around him at the display of unashamed opulence. The marquee itself was roughly the size of a football pitch, the roof draped in deep blue fabric dotted with tiny points of light so that it looked like a clear night sky. In the centre of the marquee was a dance floor surrounded by tables which had been laid with fine china, crystal and centrepieces of lush white and yellow roses. The chairs around the tables were covered with some kind of shiny gold fabric, with white satin bows tied around the backs, and there were more baskets, planters and pots of flowers than Alex had seen in one place since his mother had dragged him to the Chelsea Flower Show as a child. At the far end a band was set up on a small stage, and the musicians were busily tuning their instruments.

Spotting a long table set up near the entrance, already piled high with gifts, Alex looked at the brightly wrapped box he was holding. He turned to Damian, who was standing beside him, hands in the pockets of his trousers, quite breath-taking in his unaffected elegance. "What's in this, anyway?" Alex asked, his voice a touch gruffer than usual.

"A bottle of sixty-year-old single malt." Damian swiped a glass of champagne from the tray of a passing waitress and threw it back in one swallow before signalling for another.

Alex's jaw dropped and he held the box a bit tighter. "Sixty years? Are you serious? That must have cost a fortune."

Shrugging, Damian gulped from the glass like he was drinking cheap beer and not fine champagne. "Don't worry about it; it's not like I can't afford it."

Alex scowled at the flippant reply, but Damian was too occupied scanning the assembled guests to see his friend's disquiet. Before Alex could say anything, Damian spotted someone he knew and took off, depositing the empty glass as he went. Sighing, Alex took the bottle of whisky and set it down on the table with the other gifts. Damian had been acting weird all day. After disappearing down to the stables for hours on end, he'd turned up late for lunch and given an uncanny impression of a moody, monosyllabic teenager before holing himself up in his room for the rest of the day saying he had important business calls to make.

If he didn't know better, Alex might think his friend was trying to avoid him, but that made as much sense as Damian being unable to meet his eyes earlier in the kitchen. Still, Alex couldn't banish the unease simmering in his stomach.

"You look like you could use a drink." Alex turned to find Romilly holding out a glass of champagne to him. "Consider this an entrée until I can find something stronger."

Alex huffed a laugh. "Aren't you supposed to be all responsible and *mumsie* these days?"

"Not tonight, sweetie." She grinned and clinked the rim of her glass against Alex's. "Helen and Martha are taking care of the bread-snapper tonight, and I plan on making the most of it. First, I'm going to drink until I want to throw up; then I'm going to dance until I fall down. And *then* I'm going to drag my gorgeous husband to the nearest semi-private place and ravish him until *he* falls down."

"Oh goody, just like the old days!" Michael came up behind his wife, wrapped a solid arm around her waist and planted a noisy kiss on the side of her neck.

"Please stop," Alex grimaced, feigning distaste. "I've known this woman since she was nine years old; to me she'll always be the funny little thing with pigtails who smelt like treacle syrup."

Romilly smacked Alex on the arm and Michael snickered. "Pigtails? Oh, I think I might like to see those."

"Pervert," she retorted, elbowing her husband in the stomach, though from the sparkle in her eye Alex could tell she wasn't nearly as scandalised as she wanted to sound. Her eyes widened then, and she emitted a little squeak of delight. "Oh look, it's Will."

Alex turned to see a man coming towards them, smiling warmly. Will Havelock was a good-looking man in his early thirties, with dark brown hair that had a tendency to fall over his eyes and an easy smile. He was Grayson's nephew, and a much-loved cousin to Damian and Romilly.

"Romilly, you thing of beauty, ditch this dullard and run away with me." Will stopped to press a kiss to Romilly's cheek.

"I think your wife might have something to say about that," Romilly replied, gesturing to where Grayson was hugging Will's wife, Felicity.

"Not to mention me," Michael growled a mock threat, extending his hand to Will in welcome.

"So, we're destined to be star-crossed lovers." Will placed a hand dramatically over his heart, mouth quirking at the corners. When he turned to Alex his smile widened. "Alex, I'm glad to see you're back with us. Africa clearly agreed with you, you're looking very well."

Alex's chest only tightened a little, and his smile didn't feel too forced. "Thanks, Will, it was a very rewarding experience."

"Where's Damian? Probably at the centre of a clutch of pretty girls now that he's back on the market?" Will laughed and was joined by Michael and Romilly —

though Romilly's laughter was softer, more reserved, and she looked up at Alex from under her lashes.

Alex took a sip of his champagne and glanced around the marquee, hoping his discomfort didn't show on his face. It was everything he could manage not to choke on his drink when his gaze came to rest on Damian—he'd always had an unerring knack for finding the man in the most crowded of rooms—and saw that he was talking with Imogen, his first wife. They were standing close together, his hand resting casually on her hip while she straightened his bow tie.

It wasn't exactly a shock to see Imogen at the party; her family and Damian's had been friends for generations, and, even though they had been divorced for nearly ten years, Damian and Imogen had never stopped caring for each other. But it never got any easier for Alex to see them together. There was a part of him that believed Damian and Imogen belonged together, and one day they would find their way back to each other.

Just the thought was enough to make Alex feel nauseated. Did he have the fortitude to stand up with Damian and watch him commit himself to someone else again? He'd been best man for Damian three times, and a little bit of him had died each time. Alex just didn't think he had it in him to do it again.

A soft touch on his hand brought Alex out of his tortuous thoughts. He looked down to see Romilly watching him with a gentle expression.

"He's not in love with her, you know," she said quietly, as if she'd been reading his mind, her blue eyes, so like her brother's, wide and imploring. She bit her lip and looked away for a second, as if she was having some difficulty speaking. "Just...please be patient with him."

Alex frowned in confusion. "Patient? I don't understand." Michael and Will were deep in conversation about something, so they could offer no clarification.

"I can't... Give him time, Alex, please?" Romilly was looking distinctly nervous now, and without another word she squeezed Alex's hand and moved away.

Thoroughly baffled, Alex watched her hurry away to greet some guests. Give him time? Be patient? What on *earth*?

Chapter Eight

Damian could feel Alex's eyes on him from the other side of the marquee. It made his skin prickle and his gut tighten. He knew he'd been acting like a bastard all day, avoiding Alex, lying to him about making business calls just so he could lock himself up in his bedroom and hide, like a frightened child.

The truth of it was that he *felt* like a frightened child. These feelings he had for Alex were so new, so unexpected. He'd spent most of the day ricocheting from one emotion to another, afraid to examine such a fundamental alteration to who he thought he was, cursing the Fates for playing fast and loose with his life, and even resenting Alex himself for bringing about this sea change by his very existence.

But, after hours of denial, confusion and anger, he kept coming back to the same question — did his shock lie in this supposed change, or in the fact that these feelings had always been there, inside him, but he had been too blind or stupid to see them?

"Damian? *Damian?*" The sound of Imogen's voice dragged Damian back to the present, and he found his ex-wife watching him with a tilt of her auburn head, violet eyes narrowed in puzzlement.

"Sorry, darling, were you saying something?" He smiled widely, but instinctively knew Imogen saw right through it. Only Alex knew him better than Imogen.

"We've been talking for less than ten minutes and I've lost your attention twice already. Where do you keep going?" There was concern in her question.

He considered laughing it off, telling her she was imagining things, but he knew she'd hear the lie in his words and had no wish to worry her further. "I have something on my mind, love. Something I have to work out; and nothing you can help with," he added, knowing that would be the first thing she asked.

"Does it have anything to do with Alex looking like someone stole his puppy?" Imogen arched one finely plucked eyebrow, and Damian, in spite of the turmoil raging in his chest, had to laugh.

"You see too much, woman, you always did."

"And you, my darling, have been walking around with your eyes closed for far too long." There was no bite in her words, and she reached out to touch his arm gently. "Come on, we need to talk. Grab a bottle of champagne, I've a feeling we may need it."

With a mixture of dread and curious anticipation, Damian followed his ex-wife from the marquee, picking up an unopened bottle and two glasses as he went.

It was a surprisingly warm evening for so early in June, a crescent moon lazing in a star-sprinkled sky that was far more beautiful than the man-made replica in the marquee. Damian easily caught up with Imogen, but allowed her to set their course. They walked together in silence for a few minutes, around the back of the house and through the formal gardens, their feet crunching on the gravel paths neatly laid out between the flower beds, to the stone fountain that was the centrepiece.

When Imogen looked at the low, curved wall surrounding the fountain and then at her flimsy red evening gown, Damian smiled. He put down the champagne and glasses, removed his dinner jacket and draped it over the wall.

"My lady."

"So gallant." Sitting, Imogen patted the place beside her. "Tell me everything."

Damian sucked in a deep breath, lowered his head and ran a hand over the back of his neck. Tell her? Shit, it was one thing to admit the truth to himself, however obliquely, or to make no denial to Romilly, but to actually say it, to speak the words out loud... His heart was beating uncomfortably quickly again, and he wondered if this was to be the norm from now on. He sighed, shaking his head, and sat beside Imogen.

"I have recently, very recently, been thinking... feeling..." He paused, scrubbed a hand through his hair, dragged it over his face. Christ, this was hard. Unable to sit still, he got to his feet and turned to face the fountain. Water arced from the mouths of cherubs to collect in a reservoir at the bottom and lights set around the base cast an eerie blue-green glow, making the area around them shimmer surreally. "I think I have...feelings for Alex."

"I know, sweetie." Imogen reached up to take his hand, her skin cooled by the night air.

Damian looked at her, shook his head. "No, I mean *feelings*. He's my best friend and I've always loved him, but this is different; this is...*more*."

"Sweetie, I *know.*" Imogen squeezed his hand and smiled fondly. "I think I've always known."

Damian withdrew his hand and took a step back, frowning. "What do you mean, you've always known? Since when?"

A soft laugh escaped Imogen, but Damian knew she wasn't mocking him. She stood, moving so that she was right in front of him, and laid her hands on his chest. "I think I knew before I even married you, but I was so mad about you I chose not to see it. Something we have in common, I think?" It sounded like a question, but Damian knew it to be more of a statement of fact. "There's something about you when Alex is around; a lightness of spirit, a sense of contentment that's never there otherwise. I believe you are only truly happy when you're with Alex."

He opened his mouth to deny it, to tell her she was imagining things, that she had lost her mind; but the words wouldn't come. The truth of it struck him like a blow. But, where a physical strike would bring pain, this brought a kind of clarity, as though the thoughts that had been careering around in his brain had suddenly settled to form a recognisable pattern.

"I need a drink." Sitting down heavily on the edge of the fountain, Damian reached for the bottle of champagne and peeled off the foil around the top.

Imogen picked up the glasses and sat beside him. "Champagne does seem in order."

"It does?" Damian twisted off the cork with a muted pop and filled the glasses Imogen held out.

"Of course. It's traditional to celebrate with the fizzy stuff." With a smile she clinked her glass against his.

Damian shook his head. "What on earth would I have to celebrate right now?"

"Are you kidding?" She looked at him like he'd suddenly sprouted a second head. "After years of endlessly searching, all those wives, all those women, you finally *know*. You've had a fucking epiphany, my love. You're finally realising that the one you've been searching for has been right there in front of you this whole time. You are arse over tits in love, and, if that's not something to celebrate, then I don't know what is."

Damian blanched. In love. With Alex. He was prepared to admit to feelings, to thoughts, but to put a label on them... Love. *In* love. It was so huge, so terrifying, and ultimately a truth so glaring in its brightness that it would not be denied. "I am so fucking screwed."

"Oh, darling, this is a good thing. Love is a good thing." Imogen leaned close and rested her forehead against his temple, then lifted her free hand to lightly stroke the back of his neck.

Emotion welled up in Damian's chest, raw and unexpected. "I do love him, more than I've ever allowed myself to admit. But..." He had to cough to clear his throat of the lump that had formed there. Imogen continued to offer silent, gentle encouragement. "What the hell do I do now? Every time I look at him it's like an assault on my senses. I can't go through my life like that, my heart would never stand the strain, and not seeing him, well that's just not an option. It's like...something's missing when he isn't there, like I'm just going through the motions."

"You should tell him," she said.

Damian's heart actually seemed to stop for the space of a couple of beats. "Tell him? That's...no, no, I couldn't. What if he doesn't... He's never given any indication that he sees me as anything more than a friend. It would ruin everything."

A puff of breath warmed his cheek when Imogen laughed softly. "When exactly was he supposed to give you this indication, love? In between wives? Perhaps at that point in the service where the vicar asks if anyone has any objections to the marriage? He's had every reason to believe that you are one hundred per cent straight, so he sure as hell wasn't going to tell you about his big gay feelings. I really think you need to talk to him."

In spite of the urgent insistence in her voice, Damian shook his head determinedly. "I can't; it's too much of a risk. If he doesn't want me like that, I could lose him altogether." Oh God, just thinking about it was enough to make him feel sick.

Imogen leant back and sighed, then took the glass from his hand and set it down with her own beside the bottle. "Come on, let's get back to the party before we're missed. Wouldn't want to set tongues wagging." She got up and held out her hand to him.

Surprised at her giving in so easily, Damian got to his feet, picked up his dinner jacket, shook it out and slung it over his shoulder. They made their way back to the marquee in silence, the sounds of music and laughter getting louder the closer they came. They were crossing the lawn, Imogen on her tiptoes to prevent the heels of her sandals from sinking into the soft earth, when she suddenly stopped and moved to stand in front of him, her body close to his.

Damian frowned. "What...?" But she cut off his words simply and effectively by pressing her mouth to his. He gasped into the kiss and his hands clutched at her upper arms in surprise. It ended as quickly as it had begun, and when she stepped back there was a glint of mischief in Imogen's eyes.

"If you really want to know how he feels, then open your eyes and look. *See*." She pointed surreptitiously over her shoulder.

Still frowning, Damian looked, and what he saw stole the breath from his lungs.

Standing just outside the entrance to the marquee, Alex looked like he was frozen to the spot, the expression on his face thrown into stark relief by the lanterns hanging on either side of the entrance. Surprise, distress, hurt; they were all there, marring his handsome features. Damian saw it and it struck a chord in him—he'd felt it all that very morning when he'd walked into the kitchen and been confronted with the flirtatious atmosphere between Alex and Jude. Was Alex's stomach churning with jealousy, too?

I really have been walking around with my eyes closed, Damian thought, feeling foolish, excited and terrified all at once.

Chapter Nine

After witnessing Damian and Imogen sloping out of the party with a bottle of champagne, Alex called upon fifteen years of practice to suppress the ache in his chest, paste on a smile and participate in the celebration. He mingled with the other guests, chatted with Will about his work as an environmental consultant for the government, and Michael about the PR company he and Romilly ran together. He danced with Romilly and Naomi, and spent much longer than he was comfortable with talking about his time in Africa. It amazed him that so many people he'd never met seemed to know so much about him.

When he could no longer smile without feeling like he was having a stroke, he decided to escape for a bit, and slipped out of the marquee. The very last thing he needed to see was Damian and his ex-wife sharing oxygen on the lawn.

A kind of panic threatened to swamp Alex, and he needed desperately to be somewhere else. There was no way he could conceal his feelings from Damian or Imogen right then; he felt too raw, too exposed.

Moving quickly, he turned in the opposite direction and strode across the lawn to the house. The front doors had been left unlocked to allow party guests access to the facilities, so Alex went inside. The house was quiet, his footsteps echoing in the main hallway as he crossed to the library. He was grateful to find it empty and slumped down on one of the long, floral print sofas flanking the big stone fireplace.

It was actually happening, the thing he had dreaded most—Damian and Imogen were getting back together. It didn't surprise Alex—he'd been expecting it for as long as he'd been dreading it—but, Jesus *Christ*, it hurt. Alex let his head fall back against the sofa and closed his eyes to fight the sting of tears. He had to pull it together. He'd done it before; he could do it again.

It had never felt so much like the end of hope before.

A bitter laugh escaped him. As if there had ever really been any hope. God, he was a world class fool.

"Alex, are you okay?"

The sound of Damian's voice startled him, and his eyes snapped open as he straightened on the sofa. Damian was standing just inside the doorway, his jacket hanging from one hand, bow tie loose and the top two buttons of his shirt undone. He looked magnificently dissolute. Alex's cock stirred at the sight and he had to swallow a groan.

"I'm fine." Alex got to his feet and wandered, as casually as he could manage, to stand in front of a bank of bookshelves. He knew from past visits that the library held everything from first edition classics to the latest paperbacks, but he couldn't have focused on a single title right then if his life had depended on it. "I just needed a break from the party; that's quite a lively crowd Naomi's gathered."

"Yes, she does know some...colourful people. I doubt Pa knows even half the people here tonight, but he's sure to get some decent presents. Naomi likes people with fat wallets." From the corner of his eye, Alex saw Damian drop his jacket over the back of one of the sofas and tuck his hands into his pockets. He moved to stand in front of another set of bookshelves, his posture stiff.

"So, I—uh, I suppose congratulations are in order?" Alex's throat seemed to tighten around the words.

"For Pa, you mean? Yes, I suppose they are, although sixty isn't all that old these days, is it?" Damian asked. He removed one hand from his pocket and ran his index finger along the spine of one of the books. He had long, slender fingers. How many times had Alex wondered how it would feel to have those fingers on his skin? To draw that index finger into his mouth and suck on it?

Heat invaded Alex and he had to turn away for fear that Damian would see the swell of his interest pressing against the front of his trousers. He went to the window where he could see the glow of the lights from the marquee and hear the muted sounds of the party. "Actually, I was talking about you and...Imogen." How was it possible to feel the searing heat of desire and the icy hand of despair at the same time?

"Alex, what you saw on the lawn, it wasn't... It wasn't real." Damian sounded more hesitant than Alex had ever heard him.

Alex frowned, but continued to face away from his friend. "It wasn't real? It looked real enough to me."

"Yes, well, I suppose that was Imogen's plan." Damian was moving around now; Alex could hear his footsteps, muffled as they were by the thick rug on the floor. "I—I think she thought she was helping."

"Helping? I don't understand." Alex turned to find Damian pacing the floor, dragging a hand through his thick hair.

"No, nor did I, not for a long time. It was all right there in front of me, but I didn't get it. I *chose* not to."

Alex's frown deepened. He wasn't sure if Damian was talking to him or to himself.

"But now..." Damian stopped pacing and turned to face Alex. "The blinkers have finally fallen away. It was Africa, you see, the catalyst. God, when I think about what might have happened I feel sick to my stomach. But even that took a while to sink in. I don't even recognise an epiphany when it practically bites me on the arse." The laugh that exploded from Damian had an almost hysterical edge to it.

"You're not making a bit of sense, Damian." Alex moved closer to his friend as concern took precedence over all other emotions. "Are you all right?"

Damian's eyes widened, and his chest was rising and falling as if he were having difficulty breathing. "Well, I rather think that depends on you."

"On me?" Alex was starting to feel like he'd fallen down the damn rabbit hole.

"Yes, you. Only you." Damian nodded, his expression a perfect mixture of doubt and anticipation. "You see, I think we're on the same page, finally. If I really saw what I think I saw on your face when Imogen kissed me out there."

Alex's chest suddenly felt tight. "What—what exactly did you see?"

There was a long pause. Damian watched Alex intently, took a deep breath as if to brace himself and asked, "Were you jealous, Alex?" It was asked quietly, Damian's voice filled with uncertainty.

Alex felt the blood drain from his face. *Oh my God, he knows, he knows.* The urge to run was almost overwhelming, but his limbs felt leaden and he doubted he could have moved if the house had been burning down around him. "Damian…" Should he apologise? How did you apologise for falling in love with your best friend?

I think we're on the same page, finally. Damian's words pierced the fog of panic engulfing Alex and his heart stuttered. It couldn't be. "Damian?"

Damian took a step closer to Alex, slow, tentative. "Were you jealous, Alex? Does it hurt you to see me with someone else?" Another step closer, and Alex could feel the warmth emanating from Damian's body.

It was getting hard to breathe. It was a cruel joke, it had to be. Damian couldn't possibly be saying… But Damian was not a cruel man. He was a good man, a kind man. A *brave* man. Hope—that most treacherous of emotions—flared to life in Alex. Could it be…was it possible that Damian was taking the step Alex had never dared to? The lie was on Alex's lips. *Deny it, just in case.* But he found himself nodding, and when he spoke his voice was little more than a hoarse whisper. "It tears the heart out of me."

In the silence that followed, the air between them seemed to shimmer. Alex half expected to wake up at any moment in a cold sweat. It wouldn't be the first time he'd dreamt about Damian, but never like this. To wake up now and have this hope snuffed out would be the cruellest thing of all, and infinitely more painful than his dreams of Africa.

When Damian lifted a hand and laid it softly on Alex's cheek, Alex sucked in a sharp breath. He barely noticed the trembling of Damian's hand for the shaking of his own body. Every second that passed seemed to stretch on unbearably, as Damian closed the last few inches between them and their lips met for the first time.

It was the merest caress, barely even a kiss, but Alex felt the contact from his mouth to his toes to his soul. Alex gripped Damian's taut biceps and his lips parted automatically. After the briefest of hesitations, Damian deepened the kiss. He opened his mouth and the tip of his tongue touched Alex's. Someone moaned — Alex had no idea who — and Damian slid one hand around to the back of Alex's head, buried his fingers in the hair there and tugged just this side of painful.

Desire surged through Alex's veins, chasing his blood to settle hot and heavy between his legs. Damian thrust his tongue deep into Alex's mouth and the pleasure centre of Alex's brain threatened to overload. Damian tasted like champagne and toothpaste, his tongue, both rough and smooth, searched Alex's mouth, twined with his own tongue and sucked it into the dark heat of Damian's mouth.

A groan rumbled up from Alex's chest and his fingers dug into Damian's arms. He tore his mouth from Damian's and dragged in a great gulp of air. "I — I can't..." It seemed that words were beyond Alex. It was everything he could do simply to breathe.

Damian frowned. "You don't want this?" Alex couldn't help feeling a thrill at the disappointment in the man's voice.

"No, I... What I was going to say was I can't believe *you* want this." Alex's gaze ran over the beloved face in front of him. Damian really was the most beautiful man he had ever seen.

A smile, just a touch shy, kicked up one side of Damian's mouth. "Give me your hand," he said.

Alex loosened his grip on one of Damian's arms and did as he asked. Damian trailed his fingers over the back of Alex's almost reverently. "You have beautiful hands; healer's hands." He curled his fingers around Alex's hand and brought it to his own chest. Moving slowly, his eyes never leaving Alex's, he drew Alex's palm down his body so that Alex could feel every hard curve and dip of Damian's torso.

When his fingers touched the waistband of Damian's trousers, Alex forgot to breathe altogether, and when Damian silently encouraged him to curve his palm around the hard thrust of his arousal, Alex knew that if he never drew another breath again that would be just fine. Damian *wanted* him. It was the fulfilment of fifteen years of wishing and hoping. What was breathing compared to that?

Chapter Ten

Hunger raged through Damian at the first taste of Alex. He wanted everything. He wanted to touch and taste, he wanted to know Alex as he'd never known him—as he'd never known anyone. He felt alive, as if charged with electricity. His skin prickled with it, his fingers tingled where they touched Alex—his jaw, slightly rough with stubble, his hands, strong and capable. A shiver ran through Damian. How would those hands feel on his naked body?

It should have felt odd, strange, to be thinking like this about the man who had been his best friend for nearly half his life, but Damian couldn't question the reaction of his own body. He was painfully hard, his cock pressing against the zipper of his trousers eagerly, urgently, and his whole body felt flushed, as though he had a fever.

Alex's fingers closed around the bulge of Damian's clothed erection, and Damian shuddered, tilting his hips to press closer. "Do you believe me now?" Damian asked, voice husky with arousal and need.

"I'm getting there," Alex replied. He still sounded a little stunned, but his pupils were blown wide, almost eclipsing the irises, fairly broadcasting his own interest in matters.

"Will you..." Damian's voice broke as a knot of nerves formed in his throat. It was neither a point of pride nor shame for him that he had been with more women than he could count, but he had never even considered doing anything with a man. He felt in that moment as uncouth as a teenager embarking on his first encounter.

Alex's hand, the one that had been gently caressing Damian's hardness, moved back up his body to cup his cheek. "What? Tell me. Surely there's nothing left that we can't talk about?" His thumb moved slowly over Damian's cheekbone in a way that was both soothing and stirring.

Coughing to clear his throat, the heat of embarrassment touching his cheeks, Damian shook his head. "No, nothing. I—I want you to come upstairs with me, but...well, I'm worried that, once we get there, I won't know what the hell to do." He laughed, but it sounded hollow, echoing with his unease.

Alex didn't laugh, but he did smile, a smile filled with so much reassurance and affection that it squeezed at Damian's heart. "Do you have any idea how long I've wanted you? You think you're nervous? I've just been granted the one thing I thought would never be within my reach; guess how nervous I am. But, above all else, we're best friends. We've seen each other through some tough times. This should be a breeze."

Amusement and relief bubbled up in Damian. "God, no wonder your patients adore you; I bet you have an incredible bedside manner."

Alex's wink was outrageously lewd. "Why don't we go upstairs and find out?"

Right then, in that moment, Damian knew without a shadow of a doubt that he was truly and completely in love for the first time in his life. Stepping back, he held out a hand that was only trembling a little. "Why don't we?"

Alex took Damian's hand, lifted it and touched his lips to Damian's knuckles. "Lead the way."

They left the library together and climbed the stairs side by side, fingers tightly entwined. Damian's heart was beating so hard in his chest that he was certain Alex must have been able to hear it, and his anxiety seemed to be keeping pace with his arousal. But he never for a second considered stopping, turning back. As Alex had said, they were best friends and they were in this together.

Reaching the landing, Damian headed in the direction of his own bedroom and guided Alex inside, taking a little longer than necessary to lock the door behind them before turning to face Alex.

His lingering uncertainty must have shown on his face, because Alex stepped closer, smiling softly. "Why don't you let me take the lead tonight?" When Damian nodded, Alex leaned in and pressed his lips to Damian's.

This Damian could do. He loved kissing, always had, and kissing Alex added an emotional dimension that was as intense as his physical reaction. Lifting his hands, Damian curled them around Alex's head while Alex's hands tightened on Damian's hips. Damian tilted his head to the side to get a better angle and opened his mouth, slipping his tongue out to run it over Alex's lower lip.

A low groan escaped Alex and his own lips parted, his tongue meeting and tangling with Damian's. Oh God, it was so good. Alex tasted so good, his lips firm but yielding, his tongue forceful but not forcing. They were breathing harshly in no time, clutching at each other, pressed so close that nothing so much as a chink of light or a breath of air could find space between them. Alex moved a hand round from Damian's hip to smooth over his backside and Damian tore his mouth away with a growl.

"Fuck!" He'd never been this hard or this close to the edge so quickly even when he *was* an uncouth teenager. Alex's hands on him...dear God, it felt incredible. But he wanted more. He wanted skin on skin. His fingers itched to touch Alex and his flesh was begging for Alex's caresses. "Clothes...too many."

Alex was flushed with lust, pupils once more blown wide. "Yes, *God yes.*" He brought his hands around to Damian's front and began to fumble with the small studs of his dress shirt, a little V of concentration between his eyebrows.

Leaning in on impulse, Damian touched the tip of his tongue to the small crease, the flavour of warm, salty damp skin exploding on his tongue. Alex laughed and dipped his head to nip at Damian's earlobe with his teeth. Damian's gasp turned to a heartfelt groan when Alex pushed Damian's shirt off his shoulders and slid his hands down to rest on Damian's chest, thumbs brushing his nipples.

"You're beautiful," Alex whispered against Damian's neck, trailing light kisses from his ear and down his neck to the hollow at the base of his throat. Goosebumps broke out on Damian's skin and his nipples hardened into tight little buds that pushed eagerly against Alex's thumbs.

"Never been...oh, fuck! Never been called beautiful be-before." Damian dropped his hands to Alex's shoulders, fingers gripping—probably too tightly— when Alex ducked his head and took one nipple into his mouth, dragging his tongue over it in a rough caress. Sensation swept over Damian, burning hot, searing him to the bone.

"I find that very hard to believe. You dated a lot of smart women, and none of them were visually impaired, to my knowledge." Still moving south, Alex slowly, so slowly, lowered himself to his knees in front of Damian and tilted his head back to smile up at him. He dragged his fingers down over Damian's torso, scoring the ridges of his abs lightly with his nails and coming to rest on the waistband of his trousers.

Damian swallowed convulsively and looked down the length of his body to the man before him. Alex's sharp cheekbones were stained red, his blue-green eyes heavy with unconcealed desire and his dark hair was mussed from Damian's fingers. *Beautiful.* Alex was the very personification of the word. Damian laid a hand on Alex's head, letting the soft strands of his hair sift through his fingers as the warmth of love bloomed in his chest. "Thank God for you."

"Tell me what you want," Alex said quietly, sweeping his index finger back and forth across the strip of skin just above Damian's waistband as he ran the tip of his tongue over his full lower lip.

Damian's gaze tracked the movement of Alex's tongue and his stomach seemed to flip over. He brought his fingers to Alex's mouth, pressed his thumb against his bottom lip and almost came right then when Alex touched his tongue to the pad of his thumb. He could feel his heart beating strong in his chest, as though he was feeling it for the first time.

"I want everything. I want to take the rest of my life and get to know every little thing there is to know about your body and your heart and your mind. But right this minute..." Damian paused, dipped his thumb into the moist depths of Alex's mouth. "Right now I want your mouth."

Alex's nostrils flared and he dragged in a breath, blinking slowly. Without a word he began to undo Damian's trousers, each brush of his fingers against Damian's skin like a brand. When he had them open, Alex pushed the trousers over Damian's hips and down his thighs, leaning in to press his face to the rigid thrust of his cock, covered only by the thin cotton of his boxer briefs. Damian gulped audibly and wondered if his knees were going to give out on him. Alex's breath was hot even through the underwear, and, as he watched, Damian saw a damp spot begin to spread over the grey fabric around the head of his prick.

"Please, Alex." Was that really his voice? He didn't recall it ever being that deep or desperate.

Alex glanced up at him, smiling. "Been a while, love?" His fingers curled around the elastic waistband and began to slide it slowly down.

Breathing in shallow pants, Damian clenched his fists at his sides to stop him from grabbing at Alex. He watched, fixated, as Alex freed him from his shorts, saw his cock spring free and point almost unerringly at Alex's mouth. Alex licked his lips and Damian groaned out loud.

"I've wondered what you'd taste like so many times," Alex said, and his voice sounded rusty. He lifted one hand and curled his fingers around Damian's shaft, looking at it like it was the greatest gift ever. "You fit perfectly in my hand; somehow I always knew that you would."

"Jesus, Alex!" Damian was hanging on to his composure by a thread. His cock was leaking pre-cum freely and every muscle in his body felt tight enough to snap. He was ready to beg and plead, to promise anything if Alex would just give him the release for which his body was crying out, but his words became nothing more than jumbled nonsense when Alex wrapped those lips—those wonderful, marvellous lips—around the head of his cock and swept his agile tongue around it.

Pleasure flared incandescent in Damian's brain and radiated though his body. His hips bucked reflexively, pushing him deeper into Alex's mouth. If he'd had the ability to form a coherent sentence he would have apologised, but Alex didn't seem to mind. In fact, he opened his mouth wider and took Damian in farther still, until his lips met the hand wrapped around the base of Damian's prick. When Alex's free hand came up to cup his balls, Damian shuddered and muttered a string of curses. His sac pulled up tight against his body, his back arched and his orgasm ripped through him like a tornado, taking his knees out from under him so that he collapsed in front of Alex, lightheaded, breathless and completely wasted.

"Holy fuck... That was..." Unable to hold his head up, Damian let it fall forwards, pressing his forehead to Alex's. He struggled to get his breathing under control, peripherally aware of Alex stroking his back. "I—I don't know if I should worship at your feet or kick your arse right now."

Startled laughter burst from Alex. "Kick my arse?"

Damian lifted his head, smiling wearily. "If you'd told me you could do *that*, I would have embraced my inner gay a long time ago."

"Your *inner gay?*" Alex laughed like it was the funniest thing he'd ever heard.

Damian grinned and aimed a half-hearted punch at Alex's arm, then brought his hands to rest on Alex's thighs. When Alex emitted a soft gasp, Damian frowned and looked down. A frisson of residual desire shivered through him when he saw that Alex was still hard, his cock — a rather impressive-looking bulge — pressing insistently against his zipper.

Slowly, a little hesitant again, Damian slid his hand up Alex's thigh until the very tips of his fingers brushed against him. "Why...uh, why don't you let me take care of that?" He could feel the heat of a blush in his face, but the desire to give Alex at least some of the pleasure he'd bestowed on Damian far outweighed any embarrassment.

"Maybe we could move to the bed?" Alex asked, trailing the backs of his fingers down Damian's cheek. "I don't know about you, but my knees aren't quite what they used to be."

Damian huffed a laugh and allowed Alex to help him to his feet.

Chapter Eleven

Stretched out on the huge bed, heels digging into the thick, down quilt, Alex reached back and braced his hands against the headboard. His heart was thundering, sweat misted his skin and every cell in his body was screaming for release. This might be a new experience for Damian, but, holy *fuck*, the man was a fast learner.

At that moment Damian was dragging his tongue along the inside of Alex's thigh, leaving a hot, damp trail, curving around to his hip and back down again, close enough to Alex's achingly hard cock that it brushed lightly against Damian's stubble-roughened jaw. Alex tried to twist his hips, to get more pressure on his erection, but Damian simply snickered and drew back, the blue eyes that met Alex's teasing. "Problem, love?" he asked, grinning like the devil he was.

"Fuck you," Alex grated out. "You're killing me here."

Damian tut-tutted. "It's true what they say, then. Doctors really do have the worst patience."

Groaning at the lame joke, Alex pressed his head back into the pillow. *Dear God, I love this man with everything that I am, but if he doesn't get a fucking move on I'm going to kill him with my bare hands!*

Damian's hands were sure as they moved over Alex's body, his initial hesitancy gone now. The graze of his fingertips over Alex's calves and the press of his thumbs into the hollows of his hips were like electric charges to Alex's system. His muscles jumped and quivered under Damian's touch like a current had been applied to them. When Damian moved up his body, dragging his tongue over his stomach, delving briefly into his belly button, Alex moaned and wrapped a leg around Damian's waist, using what strength he had left to pull the man closer, desperately seeking the friction that would end this delicious torment.

"You feel so good under me, Alex," Damian breathed, ducking his head to sweep his tongue lightly over first one nipple then the other. "I love the way you taste."

"Fuck, Damian, I… *Please*." Alex pushed his hips up against Damian's, his breath stuttering when he felt the renewal of Damian's arousal press against his own.

Damian ground their hips together, his own breath coming in harsh pants. "What—what do you want? Tell me…oh fuck!"

That! I want that. I want to slide my cock into you so deep I don't know where I end and you begin. I want to open your tight little hole with my tongue and my fingers, get you wet and fuck you until you forget there was ever anyone but me. That was what Alex wanted to say, to do, but he swallowed the words. Too soon. Damian wasn't ready for that yet.

"Just…fuck, keep doing that," he said instead, reaching down to grab a handful of Damian's wonderful arse, squeezing and pulling him ever closer, circling his hips.

Damian groaned and shuddered, pressing his face against Alex's neck while they humped against each other. His fingers closed in a bruising grip on Alex's hip and his teeth scraped against his neck. It thrilled Alex all the more to know that he would bear the marks of Damian's desire the next day.

The bed springs complained under them and the headboard thudded against the wall with the force of their movements. Alex clutched at Damian's sweat-soaked back, blunt nails leaving their own souvenir of the night. A litany of curses spilled from Alex's lips. Pre-cum spread between their bodies, slicking them, a natural lubricant for their throbbing pricks.

"I'm coming! Oh, *Jesus Christ.*" Alex clasped Damian's hair in a convulsive grip, digging his heels into the lower curve of Damian's arse as his cock throbbed and pulsed.

Damian was right there with him, hips thrusting forwards only to freeze as his seed joined Alex's between them, a sticky, slippery, perfect blending of their essence.

"Fucking hell," Damian groaned hotly against Alex's neck. "I think I might need medical assistance."

Alex laughed, smoothing his hands over Damian's back. "Well, lucky for you…"

"Lucky for me." Damian lifted his head. His eyelids were heavy, his smile languid. "My whole life I've never been denied anything. I've had the best of everything money could buy, but until this moment I never knew what it meant to be truly blessed."

Emotion welled up in Alex's throat and he felt the backs of his eyes sting. He lifted a tired hand and touched his fingers to Damian's mouth. "I never dreamed... I've wanted you for so long, but I never imagined..."

Damian kissed Alex's fingertips. "I didn't even know what I was searching for, but here you are; everything I didn't know I wanted. It's all in front of us now, love."

A thrill of excitement raced through Alex. "You take my breath away," he said hoarsely.

Damian smiled, his own eyes suspiciously bright, and leant down to place a kiss on Alex's mouth. "Funny, because you make me feel like I can finally breathe."

* * * *

Alex peered out through the crack in Damian's bedroom door, making sure the hallway was empty before he headed back to his own room — it wouldn't do for any of the family to see him leaving Damian's bedroom first thing in the morning, looking, and probably *smelling*, thoroughly debauched.

"The coast's clear," Alex said, turning back to find Damian sprawled out on the bed, barely covered by a thin sheet. Alex's stomach twisted with lust. It was like looking at the centrefold of *Playgirl* magazine.

"They'll all be recovering for at least another couple of hours. Come back to bed." Damian lifted the sheet, giving Alex a tantalising glimpse of his morning-hard cock.

As tempted as he was — and, Jesus, he was tempted — Alex shook his head. He didn't want to take the chance that Romilly or — God forbid — Grayson should come looking for Damian and find them together, in flagrante. Alex had no doubt that Damian would tell his family about them, but it should be in his own time, when he was prepared to answer their questions and deal with any disapproval that might come his way. Besides, if he were being honest, Alex liked having this time just for them; there would be time enough later to let in the world.

Still, looking at Damian spread out before him, all smooth skin and taut muscle, Alex felt his resolve slip. He gripped the door handle tighter in a vain attempt to resist, but, even before Damian offered him a slow, seductive smile, Alex knew he was fighting a losing battle. Shaking his head, laughing softly at his own weakness, Alex closed the door and crossed the room back to the bed. "You're going to be a demanding little bitch, aren't you?" Kneeling on the edge of the bed, Alex leant forwards, braced his arms on either side of Damian's head and brought his mouth to within an inch of Damian's.

"Oh, you have no idea." Grinning, Damian worked a hand between their bodies and grabbed Alex none too gently between the legs. "I'm going to drain you, leave you nothing but a dried out husk of your former self then move on to my next victim." He laughed, a maniacal, super-villain laugh that made Alex snort, even as he groaned and pressed into Damian's hand.

"And they say the female of the species is deadly." Alex pressed a brief, heated kiss to Damian's mouth and pushed determinedly to his feet. "I'll see you downstairs for breakfast."

"Might I suggest carbo-loading?" Damian turned on to his side, stretching his long body sinuously, a twinkle of mischief in his blue eyes.

"I'm doomed!" Making no attempt to hide the pleasure that filled him at the prospect, Alex let his gaze drag once more over Damian's gorgeous body before slipping quietly from the room and closing the door behind him.

The air was still and silent as Alex made his way back to his own room, trailing his fingers along the burnished oak of the wainscoting, as if the house itself was sleeping. At the end of the hallway, sunlight filtered through sheer curtains at a wide arched window, a promise of another fine day. Alex smiled. He fancied he would have found this day perfect even if it was blowing a gale and pouring rain.

"Well, look at you, doing the walk of shame."

Alex started at the unexpected voice, and turned to find Romilly standing at the door to the room opposite Damian's, Belle nestled in her arms, a smile Alex could only describe as gleeful playing around her mouth.

"Romilly, you surprised me." Heat flooded Alex's cheeks at the knowing look in Romilly's eyes. "You're up and about early."

"Long lie-ins are a thing of the past when you have a three-month-old demanding attention. Helen and Martha were darlings to look after her last night, but there are just some things that only a mother can provide." Stepping out into the hallway, Romilly closed the door behind her and gestured towards the stairs. "Join me for coffee?"

"Coffee and a grilling?" Alex arched an eyebrow in question.

Romilly grinned, clearly unabashed, and shrugged. "He's my big brother; it's my duty to find out what your intentions are."

"If you say so," he replied, his own lips twitching. "Give me a few minutes to have a shower and change and I'll meet you downstairs."

Escaping into his own room, he once again removed his clothes and headed for the bathroom. The water of the shower soothed muscles that hadn't been used in far too long, and Alex's smiled widened until he knew it must look positively goofy. He was glad Romilly knew about Damian and him, though he had no idea *how* she knew, and was not only all right with it, but apparently happy. He hated to think of Damian being at odds with his family because of him.

The smiled slipped a little then. Of course, Grayson still had to be told. Alex had never really been able to read Damian's father. The man seemed to epitomise the stoic, reserved Englishman. Alex couldn't begin to guess how Grayson would react to finding out that his only son was involved with another man.

Pushing the thought aside — though it left a heavy feeling in his gut — he quickly finished his shower, dried off and dressed in a fresh shirt and jeans before heading downstairs.

As he passed Damian's door it was everything he could do not to just take a peek inside. Was Damian still lounging in bed, naked but for that thin sheet barely covering miles of glorious skin? Desire lanced through Alex and his footsteps faltered when his cock twitched urgently in his jeans and his pulse kicked up a notch. A feeling of elation washed over him when he realised that he would no longer have to conceal the truth of his feelings from Damian. He could touch Damian, kiss him, press him up against a wall and rub against him until they were both moaning and coming in their trousers like teenagers. It was exhilarating, liberating and so fucking arousing that Alex had to walk downstairs slowly to give his erection time to subside before seeing Romilly again.

Chapter Twelve

"Sorry I didn't get a chance to see you before I left. Bet you're not! Want details ASAP. Love, Imogen."

Damian smiled at the text message before tucking the phone into the pocket of his jeans and opening a drawer in the dresser to take out a clean shirt. When he turned his arm he noticed that on the inside, up near his biceps, there was a patch of discolouration, like a bruise; a mouth-shaped bruise with just a hint of teeth around the edges. A thrill flashed through him at the thought of wearing Alex's mark on his skin, the shirt crushed in his fist, forgotten for the moment as his mind wandered back over the events of the last twelve hours.

Had it really only been twelve hours? He felt like his world had been turned upside down and inside out. He felt new, excited about life for the first time in far too long. He turned to look at the bed, still in a state of upheaval, and his gut tightened. Last night had been...incredible, intense, fun and hotter than Hades—everything he hadn't known was missing from his sex life.

Laughter bubbled up in his throat. Sex with Alex. My God, he should be having some kind of meltdown at the very thought, surely? A crisis of sexual identity at the very least? But, in reality, all he wanted to do was find Alex and touch him, reassure himself of the presence of the man in his life; friend, lover, *love*.

Hurriedly pulling on his shirt, not caring that it was now creased and rumpled, Damian left the bedroom and headed downstairs, an undeniable bounce in his step, and just a little clammy-palmed.

The door to the morning room was ajar, muffled voices drifting out into the hallway. Damian entered the sunny room to find Alex having breakfast with Romilly, Michael, Will and Felicity while Belle, propped up in a cushioned high-chair, was clearly fascinated by her own hands.

As he passed Alex's chair, Damian touched his fingers briefly to Alex's shoulder, before rounding the table to place a kiss on Belle's fluffy blonde hair. While bent over his niece, Damian lifted his gaze to Alex and met his lover's eyes, saw the warmth and private welcome in their blue-green depths. He smiled and dropped into the seat next to Belle.

"Good morning, loved ones. Hangovers all round, is it?" He reached for the coffee pot and filled one of the too-delicate bone china cups set out.

"Obviously not for you," Romilly said, eyeing him speculatively over the rim of her own cup. "You're looking downright perky this morning. Sleep well?"

Damian's cheeks heated, but he grinned. "Country air, good company and lots of physical activity; my needs are few and simple."

"Says the man with more clothes than Elton John," Romilly snickered, and soft laughter ran around the table. Damian shook his head, though his smile didn't falter.

"Your husband, however, looks like he hasn't slept in an age," he said, glancing at his brother-in-law. Michael's head was propped in his hand while he nursed a cup of coffee and was clearly having trouble keeping his eyes open.

"Looks like you made good on those promises of debauchery, Romilly." Laughing, Alex spread jam on a slice of wholemeal toast and took a bite. Damian watched as Alex licked his lips clean, and his dick shifted in his jeans in appreciation. Damian coughed and took a sip of coffee to moisten his suddenly dry mouth.

"I wish," Michael replied, rubbing at his temples. "I'm afraid I got a bit demob happy last night. You see, we haven't really had a night out since the baby was born, so I had a little more to drink than I planned. Rather scuppered our plans, I'm afraid." He turned an apologetic look on Romilly, who simply smiled and patted his arm.

"Never mind, love, you can make it up to me next week." She waggled her eyebrows, and, as delicate as he was clearly feeling, Michael laughed.

"What's next week?" Felicity asked, green eyes bright, eager. "Another party? I do love a good party."

Will smiled, fond and amused. "I never knew that about you." He laughed when Felicity poked him in the side.

"We're going down to Devon to visit Michael's parents for a while," Romilly explained. "We've been working so hard on the company and with Belle that we've barely had any time together. Michael's parents are looking forward to spoiling Belle, so Michael and I will have some time alone."

"I meant to ask you about your parents; they weren't able to come last night?" Damian asked. It had been in the back of his mind to enquire after Susan and Hugh, but his thoughts had been so jumbled in the last couple of days that it had simply got lost.

Michael's mouth turned down at the corners and he shrugged. "The MS has dad in the wheelchair more often than not these days. He's well, but travelling takes too much out of him."

"I'm sorry to hear that," Damian said, reaching over to squeeze Michael's shoulder.

"He's really quite well," Michael said. "He just can't get his damn legs to cooperate." He laughed, and, although there was obvious concern in his eyes, the laugh was not forced.

Felicity shifted in her seat and coughed, as though uncomfortable with the turn the conversation had taken. "I didn't see much of *you* last night, Damian. Where on earth did you get to?"

Of their own volition, Damian's eyes went to Alex, but, before he could answer, the door opened and his father and Naomi came in.

"I'd like to know that, too," Naomi said, arching her eyebrows in question, lips pursed. "You missed the speeches and the cake cutting."

Damian looked at his father as the man took his usual seat at the head of the table. "Sorry, Pa, I was…" *Humping my best friend into the mattress. Having the best orgasm of my fucking life.* Damian didn't think either of those explanations would go over too well, but Grayson held up his hand, saving him from having to continue.

"No excuses, boy. They change nothing and waste your time, and, more importantly, mine." Grayson took the tea Felicity poured for him with a nod of thanks and turned to sort through the neat pile of Sunday papers awaiting his attention.

Glad as he was that he hadn't had to come up with a lie on the spot, Damian bristled at being spoken to like a schoolboy. "Utterly unforgivable of me, I do apologise." Voice dripping with sarcasm, he laid a hand over his heart and bowed his head, but not before he saw his father's scowl or Alex's barely concealed smirk.

"You'll be back in the office tomorrow." Grayson said, opening his first newspaper. A statement, not a question.

Damian huffed a laugh, shaking his head. "Yes, Pa, I'll be back tomorrow. Actually, Alex, I was hoping I could cadge a lift back to London with you? My car's in for a service, so I came home with Pa on Thursday."

"Sure, as long as you go to the bathroom before we leave. And the first time you ask 'Are we there yet?' I will dump you by the side of the road. Understood?" Alex's eyes glinted with humour, and Damian laughed.

"You're a hard man, Jennings, but needs must and all that." He drained his coffee cup and set it down. "I'm going to head over to the stables to see Apollo for a bit. You want to come?"

Nodding, Alex reached for another slice of toast and pushed his chair back at the same time. "Of course, I love the smell of horse poop in the morning."

Grayson flicked the corner of his newspaper down to reveal his deepening scowl as he tossed a glare in Alex's direction. Naomi and Felicity regarded Alex with similar distaste, but Romilly, Will and even Michael, who was looking paler by the second, were trying, though not very hard, to hide their amusement. Belle, in an act that proved to Damian the gods really did have a sense of humour, chose that exact moment to fart at a volume that would make a drunken student proud.

For a couple of heartbeats there was absolute silence, then the room seemed to erupt with laughter. Damian was certain he even saw his father's newspaper shake a little.

"And on that note." Damian got to his feet and gestured for Alex to precede him out of the French windows. The sound of laughter followed them, only fading when they turned the corner to the back of the house and headed for the gravel path leading to the stables.

As his own amusement ebbed, a feeling of trepidation began to rise in Damian. He tucked one hand into the pocket of his jeans and brought the other up to rub at the back of his neck.

"What's wrong?" Alex asked quietly, his gaze fixed on the path ahead of them.

Damian flinched. "Hmm? What?"

Shaking his head, Alex laughed softly. "You're rubbing your neck; you do that when you have something on your mind."

A rueful smile curved Damian's lips. "I'm not going to have any secrets at all from you, am I?"

Alex grinned and bumped his shoulder against Damian's. "Not if I can help it. Come on, spill."

They came to the grove of cypress firs and Damian paused beside the stone folly, taking a moment to consider his words before he spoke. He leaned against one of the carved columns supporting the domed roof with a nonchalance he wasn't quite feeling. "I was thinking about when we get back to London. You, uh, you'll be looking for a place of your own, I suppose, away from the family home?"

There was a marble bench by the folly. It had once been smoothed to a glossy finish, but years of exposure to the elements had left the surface dull and flat. Alex walked around the bench, trailing his fingers over the rather ostentatious angel carved into the back. "Yes, I suppose I will, I'll need to find gainful employment too."

Damian nodded and swallowed to alleviate the tightness in his throat. "I was wondering, well, I thought you might like to stay at my place?" He winced at the uncertainty that laced his words. God, he sounded appallingly needy.

Rubbing his thumb over the tip of the angel's marble wing, a smile lifted Alex's mouth — small, as though he wasn't quite certain himself. "Are you asking me to move in with you?"

Damian shrugged. "We shared a place together at university and lived to tell the tale."

"Sharing and living together are two very different things," Alex reasoned, but his smile was getting wider as he moved nearer to Damian.

"Indeed," Damian agreed, his confidence growing. "No separate shelves in the fridge for a start, or half-eaten cans of beans with 'mine, do not touch' scrawled on them."

Alex nodded, moving to stand in front of Damian. "Mm, and no having to make ourselves scarce when the other is entertaining."

"No arguing over whose turn it is to scrape the ring from around the bath; I have a housekeeping service for that kind of thing these days." Damian turned so that his back was to the column and Alex was standing just inches in front of him.

"Damian." Alex leaned closer, his breath warm against Damian's mouth. "I would love to live with you."

Elation swelled in Damian's chest and he closed the small gap between them to press a kiss to Alex's mouth, wrapping his arms tightly around his shoulders.

Alex responded by dropping his hands to Damian's hips and pushing him back against the column. Damian's lips parted on a groan and he slid a hand up to spear his fingers through Alex's hair. They were both hard already, pressing urgently against each other, hands clutching, breath ragged. It was explosive, this thing between them. Damian had never experienced anything like it in his life.

He couldn't wait to find out what came next.

Chapter Thirteen

Returning to the house just before lunchtime, rumpled and sweat-stained from their horse ride, and with pieces of straw stubbornly clinging to their clothes from their more private activities in the free loose box next to Apollo's, Alex and Damian found the family relaxing on the patio outside the morning room. Seated around a big, oval, wrought iron table, Naomi had her nose buried in a copy of Cosmo, Will was slouched in his chair dozing, Grayson and Felicity were discussing some play they were both interested in seeing, and a little farther away, in the shade of a hornbeam tree, Romilly and Michael were playing with Belle.

It was a genteel, idyllic tableau, like something from a period drama. Alex couldn't help wondering if he and Damian had a place in this scene. How would the people gathered here react to finding out about his and Damian's new, improved relationship?

Seemingly unconcerned, Damian dropped with effortless grace into one of the free chairs. "I'm starving. Worked up a hell of an appetite this morning."

Alex was glad he was already flushed from his exertions, as it helped disguise the heat that flooded his cheeks at Damian's words. The man wouldn't know discretion if he fell over it in the street. Taking a seat of his own, Alex tried to glare at Damian, but he looked so self-satisfied and fucking happy that Alex found himself biting back a smile instead.

If he was being honest, Alex was feeling pretty self-satisfied and happy himself. He was in love, which was nothing new in and of itself; but in the space of a single weekend he'd discovered that the man he'd adored for nearly half his life not only loved him back, but also wanted Alex to move in with him. It was almost more than Alex could process.

"That's not all you've worked up," Naomi said, wrinkling her nose delicately. "You *are* planning on cleaning up before lunch?"

"You've spent too much time in Belgravia, my dear stepmother. Real men smell earthy and natural." Damian grinned and dragged his finger down the condensation that had formed on a pitcher of fruit juice.

"My darling stepson," Naomi said, her smile saccharin sweet. "You smell like a horse's arse. That's a little too much earth and nature for any society."

"The woman's got a point," Will added, not bothering to open his eyes.

Damian's mood was clearly irrepressible today. Instead of taking offence, he scratched his armpit and kicked Will under the table. Will snorted and tossed Damian a rude hand gesture that made Felicity frown in displeasure at her husband. Damian just smiled widely and got to his feet. "I'm off to beautify myself.

Alex, are you just going to sit around here stinking the place up? They were talking about you too, you know. They were just being polite because you're a guest."

"I've said it before and I'll say it again, you're an overgrown *child*, Stanhope." Smiling to take any bite out of his words, Alex pushed away from the table and followed Damian inside, fighting the urge to aim a smack at Damian's toned arse.

"And be quick about it," Grayson called after them. "Martha will be serving lunch soon."

Damian stuck his tongue out when they were far enough away that he wouldn't be seen, and Alex shook his head in mock exasperation, pinching Damian's backside as they climbed the stairs.

When they reached the landing, Damian crowded Alex back against the wall and nuzzled at Alex's neck. "My shower is more than big enough for two; I'll scrub your back," he offered, licking over Alex's pulse point to the hollow behind his ear.

Alex gasped and let his head fall to the side to give Damian better access. "Not clever," he said, voice shaky, regretful. "I've a feeling someone will come looking for us if we're not back in time for lunch."

Laughing, his breath hot against Alex's skin, Damian nibbled lightly on his earlobe. "That would certainly spice up the conversation at the dinner table."

"You're incorrigible." Alex ran his hands over Damian's back, fingers plucking at the damp material of his shirt. The smell of sweat and hay transported him back to the stables, and in his mind's eye he could see them, tumbling over each other in the straw, their naked bodies glistening with perspiration, straining and impatient. The memory had Alex rock hard and throbbing in his jeans, pressing his hips against Damian's as he sought release.

Damian was breathing hard and ragged. He twisted slightly so that his cock was pressed against Alex's hip, and Alex's against his. They rutted against each other, biting back moans of pleasure, fingers clutching tight enough to bruise.

"Oh, fuck!" Damian bit out. "I want you more every time we do this. I want..."

Alex tipped his head back to rest against the wall and watched Damian through hooded eyes. "What? Tell me. You can have anything."

"Jesus, Alex, you'll be the end of me." Damian's voice was rough, his eyes nearly black with lust. He eased a hand down the back of Alex's jeans, into his underwear, and slipped a finger tentatively between his arse cheeks to touch the tight furl of his opening. "I want to fuck you."

Alex's pelvis bucked and he came so hard that his vision greyed out at the edges. He leaned heavily against Damian, limbs suddenly as sturdy as warm butter. "Oh my God, you broke me," he whispered, forehead pressed to Damian's shoulder.

Huffing a laugh against Alex's jaw, Damian stroked a hand soothingly over his hair. "Yeah, I'm good. I could've been a professional."

Alex chuckled happily, lifting his head to meet Damian's eyes. "Too late for that. You're all mine now."

"You won't get an argument from me. Now, why don't we get cleaned up, grab something to eat then head back to London this afternoon?" He placed a kiss on Alex's parted lips and stepped back. "I'm rather anxious to get you alone."

"What about...?" Alex looked down and saw a wet stain spreading over the crotch of Damian's jeans.

"Oh. I was going to offer to help, but I seem to be redundant."

"Never mind that." Damian smiled. "Go on, before I change my mind and give them all something to talk about after all. I'll meet you downstairs."

Nodding, Alex touched his mouth to Damian's in a soft kiss and headed along the hallway to his own room, aware of Damian's eyes on him with every step he took.

He showered and dried off quickly, then wrapped himself in a thick blue towelling robe and left the bathroom to dress, smiling and ridiculously eager to see Damian again. The smile faltered, however, when he stepped into the bedroom and saw Grayson standing at the window, his broad shoulders silhouetted by the sun pouring in.

Hearing Alex's entrance, Grayson turned. Alex couldn't see the man's face properly with the sun behind him, but instinct told him this wasn't going to be good.

"Grayson. Is there something I can do for you?" Alex immediately felt defensive and tucked his hands into the pockets of the robe to counter the urge to cross his arms over his chest. Grayson might have him on the back foot here, but *he* didn't need to know that.

"I'd say you've done quite enough, wouldn't you?" Grayson moved away from the window. His posture was stiff and, when Alex was better able to see him, he noticed that Grayson's eyes were flinty cool and that his lips were pursed so tightly there was a white outline around them. "Do you think I haven't seen the way you look at him? The way your eyes follow him around? For years I've watched you lusting after my son. *My son!*" His eyes flashed with outrage and his hands clenched into fists at his sides.

Oh, God. Alex felt his stomach plummet. This was bad. No, this wasn't just bad; this was a fucking *shit storm*. "Grayson..." Alex took a step forwards, but stopped when Grayson threw up a hand.

"Young man, there is nothing, *nothing* you can say right now that will in any way excuse the way you have taken the trust and affection this family has offered you and twisted it into something vile and disgusting." Grayson's lip curled and he looked like he had an especially foul odour under his nose.

Alex's hackles rose at that and his spine straightened. "I don't think I like what you're implying here, Grayson."

"I don't particularly care what you do or do not like, Doctor Jennings," Grayson retorted, eyes narrowed with intense dislike.

Doctor Jennings. So, Alex was getting his full title. Grayson really was pissed off. "Perhaps you'd care to tell me exactly what I'm supposed to have done that you find so distasteful?"

Grayson sneered. "There is no *supposed* about it. My son has given you friendship and a taste of a lifestyle that would otherwise have been far beyond your middle-class imaginings. But a taste wasn't enough for you, was it?"

"What the hell are you talking about?" Anger unfurled low in Alex's gut, seeping into his bloodstream like poison.

"You know exactly what I'm talking about." Grayson moved so that he was standing right in front of Alex, bringing to bear years of practice intimidating underlings and competitors alike. But Alex didn't flinch, meeting the fury in Grayson's eyes with his own ire. He'd stared down the barrel of a fucking loaded gun while the trigger was pulled; Grayson Stanhope didn't scare him.

"Actually, I have no idea. Enlighten me." Alex tilted his chin back and saw a brief flicker of uncertainty in Grayson's eyes before it quickly disappeared.

"I know you've always wanted my son. You've spent years lying in wait under the guise of friendship, like a damn predator, until he was vulnerable enough to fall for your *seduction*." Grayson emitted a sound that was pure revulsion and turned away, as if he could no longer bear to share the same space as Alex. "He's never had good judgement where it comes to matters of the heart, and each of his failures stripped a bit more of his soul away. With this last divorce... You saw your chance, didn't you? He was at a low ebb and you just swept in with your oh-so-caring doctor routine, taking advantage and turning his head."

Alex had never been a violent man, but at that moment it took every ounce of his will not to unleash on Grayson the full force of the rage coursing through his body. For the first time in his life, Alex felt hatred for another human being. It was an emotion so foreign to him, so shocking to his system that it somewhat doused the near overwhelming need to lash out. "Damian, his name is Damian. You call him 'my son' like he's a piece of property you own, but you don't own him. He's his own man and I'm proud to say that I love him."

Laughter, ugly and cold, spilled from Grayson. "You *love* him? My God, do you have any idea how absurd you sound?"

Alex opened his mouth to retort, but the words froze on his lips when the door opened slowly and he saw

Damian standing on the other side. He looked pale, stunned, and Alex knew that he'd heard too much.

"What exactly is absurd to you, Pa?" Dear God, his voice sounded so hollow it made Alex ache. "Is it the idea of a man loving another man, or is it the fact that Alex loves *me* that you find so preposterous?"

Chapter Fourteen

"Damian…" Alex moved towards him, but Damian held up his hand to still his lover, his eyes never leaving his father.

"Well? Are you going to answer my damn question?" His throat was so tight it was difficult to get the words out.

Grayson's eyes narrowed and his shoulders squared. "Don't use that tone with me, boy." The words were spoken quietly, but the underlying threat was clear. No one spoke to Grayson Stanhope with anything less than absolute respect, and, more often than not, just a little fear.

"Just answer me," Damian demanded, his own posture so rigid that his muscles protested. Damian gave respect where it was due, but he did not, and never had, feared his father. Grayson wasn't a bully per se, but he was a man who was used to getting what he wanted, and was not above throwing his metaphorical weight about to get it. Damian's refusal to play beta male to his father's alpha had been the cause of more than one blow-up between them.

Grayson's face twisted with an expression that was equal parts pity and frustration. "Do you honestly believe this man *loves* you? Are you really that much of a fool? It never occurred to you for a second that he might have an eye on a bigger prize?"

"A bigger prize?" Damian frowned, confused for a second until the meaning of Grayson's words hit him. "Oh, my God, you think Alex is after my money?"

Grayson's jaw flexed, and Damian guessed he was gritting his teeth. "How the hell can such an intelligent man be so bloody naïve? What on earth makes you think he's so different from every woman who's passed through your bedroom door? Every one of them, save Imogen Fredericks, looked at you and saw my heir," he stated, a glint of triumph in his eyes.

"Now wait a damn minute." Alex's voice reflected the anger roiling in Damian's stomach. He was tempted to let Alex tear a strip off Grayson — God knows Grayson deserved it — but Alex had been insulted too much already, and Damian was loath to give his father a chance to aim one more derogatory word at him.

"Look, Pa, I know this must be difficult for you to take in," Damian said, trying to make his tone as conciliatory as possible, stepping between Alex and Grayson. "But what Alex and I have is real. I've known for a long time that there's been something missing in my life, and it's only very recently that I've had my eyes opened." While he wanted to avert a showdown between his father and Alex, Damian spoke with absolute sincerity; a part of him hoping that Grayson would hear and understand.

It was a faint hope. He knew it even as he thought it, but that didn't stop the disappointment clawing at him when his father's face contorted with revulsion.

"I don't give a damn what you think is real, or, more likely, what this man has made you believe." Grayson jerked his head in Alex's direction with undisguised disdain. "But I will not stand for this. I will not allow you to humiliate me, the family name, like this. It was bad enough when you were running around like a dog in heat with every money-grabbing little tart who crossed your path, and even *married* a couple, but this? *This*? No, Damian, I won't have it, do you hear me? *I will not have it.*"

Damian flinched, took an involuntary step back as though his father had actually hit him, and stared at the man, his ears ringing in the sudden silence that followed Grayson's booming tirade. Grayson's face was red with fury, his body trembling with it. Damian had seen his father angry many times — often at Damian himself. But he had never before seen this level of rage. It bordered on hatred, and it was focused like a laser on *him*.

When he felt Alex's hand on his back, Damian turned and found he had to blink a couple of times to dispel the haze that seemed to be surrounding him. "Alex, I—I think it's time we left."

Ignoring Grayson's presence, Alex lifted a hand to cup Damian's cheek, his eyes filled with worry. "Are you all right?"

Damian nodded and pressed into Alex's caress. "Let's just pack and go, yeah?"

"Let's," Alex said, and the tenderness in his voice made Damian's breath hitch.

"You've lost your mind," Grayson accused harshly. "Have you even stopped to consider how this will affect the company? In the current climate a scandal like this could be disastrous. My God, man, what you're doing is illegal in some of the countries in which we do business."

Bitter laughter spilled from Damian. "Yes, well, I think I've made it perfectly clear in the past just how I feel about that." How like his father to think of work at a time like this.

"My son, the bleeding heart liberal," Grayson sneered. "Well, it's one thing to have sympathy for the devil; it's another thing altogether to crawl into bed with him!"

"You *bastard*." Damian only realised he'd raised his fist to his father when he felt Alex's hand on his wrist, holding him back.

"Damian, no, that's not who you are." Alex smoothed his thumb over the bump of Damian's wrist bone, his blue-green eyes imploring.

Damian swallowed past the emotion in his throat and nodded. "I'll get my things." He took a step towards the door and stopped, reluctant to leave Alex alone with Grayson.

For a long moment Grayson held his ground, clearly stubbornly determined not to make anything easy for anyone.

"Well, I have no intention of driving back to London in a bathrobe, so unless you want a show, Grayson…" Alex slowly undid the belt on the robe, one eyebrow arched.

The colour rose in Grayson's face again and he made a growling sound in the back of his throat before striding from the room, throwing the door wide to the wall.

Surprised laughter escaped Damian. He lifted Alex's hand and pressed his lips to his lover's knuckles. "I'll be ten minutes, tops."

Alex nodded. "I'll be right here."

In the silence of his own bedroom, Damian leant back against the door and dropped his head into his hands. He didn't know whether to cry or scream. He'd been under no illusion that his father was going to be easy about this, but he'd hoped that the man would at least be willing to listen. The things he'd said; Damian wasn't sure which was the strongest emotion raging through him—shame, embarrassment, anger or sadness.

He thumped a fist against his thigh. Parents were supposed to want their children's happiness, damn it. *God, I sound like a whiny brat.*

Shaking his head, Damian pushed away from the door and went to the oak armoire that took up most of the wall opposite his bed. He didn't have much to pack, just a few shirts, some jeans and trousers, and some underwear. It took only a couple of minutes to stuff it all into a leather holdall, and another minute to collect his shaving kit from the bathroom, drop it in beside his clothes and zip up the bag. He was lifting the holdall on to his shoulder when the bedroom door opened and Romilly entered.

"What the hell is going on? Dad's storming around downstairs like he wants to shoot someone in the head."

"That would be me. Or Alex. Possibly both." Damian attempted a laugh, but it fell flat, because even if he had had a lifetime to examine the situation he knew he would find nothing remotely funny in it.

Romilly's eyes widened, and for a moment she looked as innocent as her daughter. "Oh my God, Dad found out you and Alex are..." She made a rather vague gesture with her hand and blushed.

That made Damian smile, even if there was a bittersweet taste to it. He shrugged. "I guess I wasn't as subtle as I thought."

Romilly laughed out loud at that. "Oh, love, I'm surprised you even know the meaning of the word."

"I'd be offended, but I can't afford to lose any allies right now." Damian paused, then lifted a hand to rub at the back of his neck, as if he could wipe away the prickle of unease tickling the skin there. "You, uh, you *are* an ally?"

She tilted her head to the side and pursed her lips. "You're really asking me that? You're my big brother and I love you. Being my big *gay* brother isn't going to change anything."

Damian dropped his bag on the floor and pulled Romilly into a tight hug. "I love you too, sweetheart." When he let her go he saw that his little sister's eyes were bright with tears. He smoothed a hand over her cheek and reached down to collect his bag. "I need to get Alex out of here before Pa's even more of a prick to him, but I'll see you soon, yes?"

"We'll get together as soon as Michael and I get back from Devon." Her smile was watery. "We can all go on a double date."

Damian nodded, not trusting his voice. He dropped a light kiss on Romilly's forehead before moving past her and heading for Alex's room, where he hesitated, resting his hand on the cool wood for a moment while he tried to get his unruly emotions back under control. He knew Alex. He knew the man was already unjustly blaming himself for this uproar, and Damian refused to feed that by letting Alex see him upset.

The sounds of raised voices reached him from downstairs – Naomi trying to calm Grayson's temper, Grayson practically incoherent in his rage, and above it all the plaintive cries of Belle, clearly distressed by hostility hanging in the air like a dark cloud. Damian's heart contracted in his chest as if being squeezed, and he closed his eyes against the rush of emotion that left him feeling momentarily raw. His hand fell limply to his side when it suddenly parted company with the door, and he opened his eyes to find Alex watching him. It was all right there in Alex's expression, the worry, the guilt and the regret.

Damian's resolve hardened. "If you say 'I'm sorry', so help me I will kick your arse, Jennings, got it?"

A smile, clearly surprised, kicked up one corner of Alex's mouth. "Yeah, and I'll just stand here and let you."

Damian held out a hand. "Come on. We're going to walk out of here together, our heads held high, and to the devil with anyone who disapproves."

Though he nodded, Damian could tell Alex was hesitant. He might not have said the words out loud, but his apology was written all over his handsome face. Determinedly, Damian linked their fingers and gave Alex a little tug to get him moving. He made no protest when Alex tightened his grip until it was verging on painful.

Grayson and Naomi were nowhere to be seen when they got downstairs, but at least Grayson had stopped shouting. Damian couldn't hear Belle either, so he guessed Michael had taken the baby outside to get her away from the poisonous atmosphere of the house. Martha and Helen were standing just inside the open doorway that led back to the kitchen. Martha smiled wanly and lifted a hand as if she wanted to reach out and touch, and Helen nodded, her eyes sad. Will stepped forwards when Damian and Alex reached the hallway and held out his hand.

"Well, I won't lie, cousin, this has surprised the hell out of me. But I wish you well." Smiling, Will shook Damian's hand and squeezed Alex's upper arm.

"Thanks, Will. That means a lot, honestly." Damian's smile was genuine, but it faded a little when Felicity sighed pointedly, turned and strode across the hallway and into the morning room, her heels clicking noisily as she went.

Will's smile turned apologetic, but Damian shook his head. "They'll either come round or they won't. I can't force them and I won't waste my energy trying. We'll get together when you get back to London, if it won't cause you problems?"

"I'll call you." There was only sincerity in Will's voice, and it heartened Damian.

He wanted to go to Martha and Helen and hug them, but he knew that any show of support for him and Alex would put the women in a difficult position with Grayson, so he simply smiled.

As they headed outside, Damian could feel the weight of Alex's silence pressing heavily on him.

They'd reached Alex's car, a silver Saab, and were putting their bags in the boot when Damian heard the front door to the house open. With a sense of dread, he turned and saw his father standing on the stone steps, forehead furrowed, eyebrows a tight, straight line.

"This is a one-way street you're setting out on, Damian. If you continue on down it there can be no turning back."

Damian's throat felt constricted and his lips tightened into a thin line. "I've finally found the path I need to be on, Pa. Can't you at least try to understand?" Yearning leaked into his voice, but it didn't seem to touch Grayson.

"Is he really worth losing everything over?" Grayson asked. His face was as cold and hard as stone. "Because that's what will happen if you go with him. You lose everything — your family, your job, your inheritance. If you leave here with him today, you leave with nothing."

Ignoring the knot of despair in his chest, Damian looked at Alex. His lover was still and quiet, lines of tension bracketing his mouth, and he seemed to be having difficulty meeting Damian's eyes. The desire to get Alex away from there, to replace that bleak expression with one of his thousand watt smiles, rose, sudden and fierce, in Damian. Turning his attention back to his father, Damian shook his head. "No, Pa, you're wrong; I'm leaving here with everything."

Chapter Fifteen

Alex felt sick to his stomach. *What the fuck have I done?* He looked in the rear-view mirror as they drove down the driveway, away from Garnet House. The old house seemed to glow in the afternoon sunlight, the windows gleaming jewel bright. It was a magnificent sight. Damian's birthright; and he was giving it up for Alex? Nausea rolled over Alex and he had to take a deep breath to keep down the little bit of food he'd eaten that day.

He could feel Damian's eyes watching him, the concern emanating from his lover practically a physical presence in the car. Alex kept his eyes on the driveway, blinking at the way the sun filtered through the leaves on the trees, flickering like a strobe light on the bonnet of the car. The gate came into view, iron lacework anchored in thick stone columns. Alex's pulse started to race and his heart thudded too fast as beads of perspiration broke out on his forehead. With a sharp, jerky movement, he pulled the car over to the side of the driveway, turned off the ignition, unlatched his seatbelt with shaking hands and threw open the door, launching himself out of the car as panic gripped him.

"Alex? What on earth?" Damian got out of the car more slowly, the frown marring his normally smooth forehead telling of his confusion.

Alex turned away, walked across the grass verge to a tree and braced his fists against the rough bark while he tried to get his breathing under control. His vision was starting to get fuzzy and his whole body was trembling. *Jesus Christ.* He hadn't had a panic attack since the early days after his return from Africa.

"Hey, what's going on here?" Damian's voice was soft; the hand that touched Alex's back gentle.

Alex shook him off and spun away, out of reach. "You have to go back. You have to go back now."

"What the hell are you talking about?" Damian took a step closer, but Alex shook his head.

"You heard Grayson; you'll lose everything. I can't let you do that, not for *me*." God, his extremities were starting to tingle now, and he had the horrible feeling that he was going to pass out.

Damian sighed, a harsh, impatient sound and came towards Alex, ignoring the hand that Alex held up to stop him. "Okay. Firstly, if there was anyone in the world that I was going to give up everything for it would most certainly be you. I want that on the record." When Alex opened his mouth to argue, Damian was the one to hold up his hand. "But the honest truth is that I'm really not giving up that much."

"I'm sorry, I must not be getting enough blood to the brain. Would you please explain that?" Damian was close now, and Alex could feel his warmth, smell the light scent of his aftershave. It was a heady combination that did nothing for the clarity of his mind.

"Grayson is pissed off right now," Damian explained, bringing his hands up to cup Alex's face. He smoothed his thumbs over Alex's cheeks and a very different kind of tingle ran through his body. "You know it drives him crazy that I have a mind of my own and refuse to let him control me. He'll either get over it or he won't. I'm not saying it won't sadden me if he really does disown me, but I can't live my life just to please my father — *I'd* go crazy that way. I won't lose Romilly, Michael or Belle, and Will is clearly not upset by this new turn. As for my inheritance — Garnet House is just bricks and mortar, love, and I don't need Grayson's money; I have my own."

Alex's heart rate was starting to settle into something more like a normal rhythm, but he still felt unsettled. "I don't know, Damian, can it really be that easy? I can't help thinking... You're all fired up right now, but what if... Once some time has passed and you've had a chance to think, you might..." Fuck, he couldn't even bring himself to say the words out loud. Just the thought of it made him ache.

"You think I'm going to regret this — us." It wasn't a question, but Damian didn't seem angry. Instead, he leaned in and pressed his forehead to Alex's. "When you told me about what happened to you out in Africa, I felt... I felt like someone had held a loaded gun to *my* head. I wasn't just *thinking* about what might have happened to you, I could *see* it, playing over and over in my head like a fucking movie on a loop. This wasn't just the concern or fear of one friend for another — I felt like someone had threatened my own life — like if anything had happened to you — if I'd lost you — I'd have lost myself, too. You want to talk about regrets? It makes me want to heave when I think that I might only have realised my true feelings for you when it was too damn late to do anything about it."

Pulling back slightly, Alex searched Damian's face for any sign of exaggeration or dissemblance, but saw only the truth in those beloved blue eyes. Love for the man before him spread through Alex, filling up every cell and atom, leaving no room for the fear and doubt that had been plaguing him since he'd walked out of the bathroom and found Grayson waiting for him.

One last thought occurred to him and he tilted his head to the side. "This isn't just another way to challenge Grayson, is it?"

Damian's eyes narrowed. "You know me better than that, Alex."

Alex smiled and lifted a hand to curl it around the back of Damian's neck, pulling him close enough to feel their breath mingling. "Yes, yes I do." He touched his lips to Damian's and felt Damian sigh into his mouth. It sounded—and felt—like part desire, part relief.

Alex was distantly aware of a faint creaking noise and recognised it as the sound of the gates opening, but he was too busy savouring the taste and feel of his lover—the silk of Damian's hair against his fingers, the hint of coffee on his tongue as it licked and swirled around Alex's—to pay very much attention until the rumbling of a truck grew too loud to ignore. They parted, glassy-eyed and slightly out of breath, and turned their heads to see half a dozen men, probably the crew come to take down the marquee, staring at them with wide eyes and slack jaws. The driver's attention was so focused on them that he seemed to have forgotten all about the couple of tons of metal under his control. Luckily, he had slowed the truck to little more than walking pace.

"Good afternoon, gentlemen, lovely day for it." Damian grinned widely and raised his hand in a hearty greeting. Every man in the truck turned his head sharply to face the road ahead and the driver stepped on the accelerator, jolting them forwards.

Damian snickered mischievously. "Well, that was fun. Shall we get going?"

"I'm going to have my hands full with you, aren't I?" Alex asked, his heart swelling with affection.

Walking towards the car, Damian looked over his shoulder and winked. "Full to overflowing, baby."

Alex snorted and shook his head. "You know, for an intelligent man, you can be incredibly dense." He followed Damian to the car and looked at him over the roof.

"Oh, really?" He arched a dark blond eyebrow, one side of his mouth twitching with amusement.

"Yes, *really*. God, man, how could you not have known I loved you? Why the hell else would I have put up with you for all these years?" There was no heat in Alex's words, and he knew without a doubt that his feelings for Damian were written all over his face. It was as if, since realising he no longer needed to conceal the truth, a mask had fallen away and he wouldn't have been able to put it back in place even if he'd wanted to.

Damian's face practically lit up. His eyes shone with pleasure and his smile was wide and bright. "I don't think I've ever been insulted quite so sweetly in my life."

"Just get in the car," Alex laughed. "I've a feeling if we hang around here much longer Grayson will set the dogs on us."

"We don't have any dogs," Damian replied. "Although Naomi and Felicity were looking pretty rabid, so maybe you're right."

Chuckling quietly, Alex ducked to get into the car, but stopped when he heard Damian say his name. When he straightened up and looked at his lover again, Damian's smile had softened and all trace of mischief was gone from his eyes.

"Just so you know, I love you, too." There was a hint of pink in Damian's cheeks, and Alex had the sudden thought that the man hadn't said those words many times in his life.

Not wanting to make Damian feel awkward or uncomfortable, Alex simply smiled and nodded. "Come on, let's go."

Relief flashed across Damian's face. "Are you okay to drive?"

Though he still felt a little shaken from the intensity of the emotions that had gripped him just moments ago, Alex nodded again. "I'm good."

When they passed through the open gates at the end of the driveway, Alex reached over and took Damian's hand. Damian squeezed Alex's fingers in return. Neither of them looked in the mirrors for a final glimpse of Garnet House before it disappeared from view.

* * * *

"What happened to the Mayfair apartment?" Alex asked, retrieving his bag from the car and following Damian into the old, red-brick building that looked like it had been some kind of factory or warehouse in a former life. It was early evening and the many Bankside bars, cafes and restaurants were filling up with people making the most of the last hours of the weekend.

Damian waved a greeting to the doorman and punched the button to call the lift. "It was a company apartment. I decided after Shannon and I split up that I wanted my own place. This isn't too downmarket for you, is it?" he asked with a smile.

Downmarket was not how Alex would describe Damian's new home. The building reeked of affluence, from the lushly carpeted and mirror-panelled lift to the original-looking artwork hanging on the walls of the hallways. "It'll do, I suppose," Alex replied, grinning.

The apartment itself was pure New York loft with exposed brick and beam, recessed lighting and glossy hardwood floors throughout the open-plan design. The windows had been restored in the small-paned style that would have been there when the building was still used for industrial purposes, except for one entire wall of glass doors that opened, concertina style, on to a wide balcony. The furnishings were clearly expensive, but understated—leather sofas in cream and brown, coffee and end tables in pale wood and glass, and neutral coloured rugs on the floor.

Alex's attention was almost immediately captured by a twelve foot by eight foot black and white photograph hanging in the dining area. The model in the picture, a leggy blonde with curves in all the right places, was nude save for a thin strip of silk draped artfully across her hips.

"What do you think?" Damian asked, coming to stand behind Alex, wrapping his arms around Alex's waist.

Alex tilted his head to the side and considered the picture for a minute, leaning back into Damian. "As an amateur photographer I think it's stunning—the light and shadow give it real depth and a kind of melancholy reality." He turned slowly in Damian's arms and smiled. "As a peek into your psyche, I'd have to say that you, my love, have been seriously overcompensating!"

Damian laughed, clearly delighted. "Fuck you, Jennings."

"Well, I'm usually more of a top, but for you? I could be flexible." Heat blossomed low in Alex's stomach and his blood rushed south to fill his cock, leaving him hard between one heartbeat and the next.

Damian blinked slowly and slipped one hand under the hem of Alex's shirt, the tips of his fingers skimming lightly over the skin at the small of his back. "Let me give you a tour of the place. We can start with the bedroom."

"Good plan." Alex's chest was tight with anticipation, and desire, never very far away when he was in Damian's presence, flared to life, bright and sharp.

Chapter Sixteen

Damian was amazed that his fingers could be so sure and steady as they worked on the buttons of Alex's shirt, while his insides were a jumble of lust, urgency and nerves. The last couple of days had gone a long way to dealing with the trepidation he'd had about having sex with another man — with *Alex* — but he was anxious that the first time they really connected should be as close to perfect as he could make it. His eyes devoured every inch of perfect bronzed skin that was revealed as he pushed Alex's shirt off and let it fall to the floor at their feet. Alex's strong, wide shoulders were smooth, but his chest was covered in dark hair, slightly coarser than that of his head, that narrowed to a point and disappeared into the waistband of his trousers.

When Damian dragged his fingers down Alex's chest, scratching through the hair, the blunt tips of his nails digging in slightly, Alex groaned and dug his own fingers into Damian's hips.

"God, Damian, I love the way your hands feel on me. I've thought about it so often, but it never felt half so good in my fantasies." Alex's voice was already hoarse with desire, and Damian could see the way his dick pushed against the zipper of his trousers.

Suddenly dry mouthed, he unbuttoned Alex's trousers and worked his hand inside to cup him through his shorts. So hot, so hard. Need lanced through Damian, making his own cock swell and beg for attention. "What did you think about, Alex?" The angle was awkward, but he gripped Alex's shaft and squeezed until Alex's hips bucked forwards.

"I—oh, fuck..." Alex's head fell back as if his neck was no longer strong enough to support it, and his eyelids fluttered closed, ridiculously long lashes feathering the tops of his cheeks. "I th-thought about you touching my nipples, pinching them, getting them hard."

Damian sucked in a ragged breath and lifted his free hand to Alex's chest. His nipples were like small brown buttons. He flicked his thumbnail over one and Alex let out a sharp cry and his prick jumped in Damian's hand. Damian smiled and repeated the action, glorying in the honesty of Alex's unreserved response. "Did you ever think about this?" Lowering his head, he touched the tip of his tongue to the same nipple and swirled it around until it was a tight bud and Alex was breathing in short, harsh pants.

"Fuck, yes." Alex brought one hand up to curve around the back of Damian's head, silently encouraging him to continue.

A small nip of teeth was greeted by a shudder from Alex, and Damian could feel dampness beginning to seep through the cotton of Alex's underwear. For long moments he devoted his mouth to tearing as many cries and moans from his lover as he could, licking, sucking, soothing first one nipple then the other, until

Alex was writhing against him, skin moist with perspiration and pleas falling from his lips.

Damian wanted Alex writhing under him, begging to be fucked, to be owned. He pushed his hips against Alex's and a guttural moan escaped him at the sweet pressure against his aching dick. "Need you, Alex. *Fuck*, need you soon." He tore at the fastenings of Alex's trousers and pushed them and his underwear over his hips. Alex was so hard that his prick was curving up towards his flat stomach.

"Soon... now!" Alex struggled frantically with his clothes, pushing them down his long legs and kicking them aside with shoes and socks. The fingers that dealt with the fastenings on Damian's shirt were remarkably coordinated, but quickly seemed to run out of patience, sending the last two buttons flying.

"Get on the bed," Damian said, both a demand and a request. Alex moved away with obvious reluctance, but climbed onto the big bed and lay back against the pillows, one arm thrown over his head, the other resting just above his cock. Damian's hands paused in the act of removing his own clothing. "Jesus, you look good enough to eat."

Alex smiled, soft and sensual. "So, what's stopping you?" He wrapped his fingers around his own cock and stroked slowly, up and down, eyes dark with need.

"Damned if I know." Moving forwards while he removed his clothes, Damian left them in an untidy trail behind him. The bed gave under his knees and Alex parted his legs, making room for Damian, welcoming him home.

"Not to kill the moment, but do you have anything we can use for lube? I haven't done this in an age, and you're pretty fucking hung there." Alex licked his lips when he looked at Damian's cock, and, as if knowing it was the centre of attention, the bloody thing pulsed and twitched.

Damian crawled up the bed, knees between Alex's spread legs, and stretched out on top of him. Their chests touched, rough on smooth, and Damian pressed a kiss to Alex's lips, hot and open-mouthed, sharing stuttered breaths, while he reached out and opened the drawer in the bedside table. His fingers scrabbled blindly for a moment before finding what he was searching for. When he dropped the tube of KY on the pillow beside Alex's head, Alex turned and gave the battered, well-used tube a speculative look. Damian grinned. "I don't have anything like as much company as people like to think, and chafing is never pleasant." He wiggled the fingers of his right hand and Alex laughed.

"C'mere." Alex wrapped a hand around the back of Damian's neck and pulled him into another kiss, sucking Damian's tongue into his mouth while he wound one leg around Damian's hips and arched up to grind against him.

Damian dragged his hand down Alex's side and gripped his thigh, lifting Alex as he pressed down. *So good*, the slide of skin on skin, the scratch of Alex's chest hair against Damian's nipples, clutch of fingers, rough rasp of tongues twining, tasting. Damian had never felt closer to another person in his life, physically or emotionally. But he wanted — *needed* — more. "Tell me what to do," he begged Alex as he released his mouth and trailed a hot, wet line down Alex's throat with his tongue. "I want... Oh God, I want everything. I want to be in you, Alex."

"Fuck, Damian, your voice... I could come just listening to you." Alex reached for the lube and pressed it into Damian's hand. "Use a lot; open me up with your fingers."

The clench of Damian's gut was almost painful and he had to remind himself to breathe when his lungs burned from lack of air. He pushed up on to his knees between Alex's thighs and took a moment to just look at the man spread out before him, all hard muscle and soft eyes. "I can't believe you're really mine." He only realised he'd spoken out loud when Alex smiled.

"I always have been." Drawing his knees up, Alex let them fall to the sides and threw his arms over his head so that he was completely open to Damian.

Damian gulped audibly and fumbled with the lid of the tube. When he finally got it open, his grip on the small tube was so tight that the viscous liquid squirted over his fingers. A flush of embarrassment heated his cheeks and he smiled sheepishly. "Well, you did say use a lot."

Grabbing hold of one of the spare pillows, Alex lifted his hips and tucked it under his backside, raising himself to give Damian better access. Damian dropped the KY on the bed beside Alex's thigh and reached out with trembling, lube-covered fingers to touch the little furl of flesh between Alex's arse cheeks. At the first, light touch of Damian's index finger, Alex gasped and his hands curled into the pillow behind his head.

"Sensitive?" Damian asked, running his finger around the opening, smiling at the way it seemed to wink at him.

"You have no fucking idea," Alex bit out, his voice like gravel. "Hurry. I want to come with you in me."

A shiver ran through Damian and his balls pulled up against his body. Fearful of hurting Alex, he pressed a single finger in to the first knuckle and groaned. *Jesus, so tight.* He imagined how it would feel to have his cock buried in the grip of Alex's body and his moan mingled with Alex's. The expression of pure pleasure on Alex's face, eyes barely slits, white teeth biting into his lower lip, spurred Damian on.

He pushed his finger in all the way, withdrew it and added a second. He forgot all about time and his own aching need as he fucked his fingers in and out of Alex, listened to the sighs and moans he emitted, watched the colour rise in his throat to stain his cheeks as he pushed down on Damian's hand. Damian's prick was throbbing and desperate for attention, but Alex looked so pretty like this, wanton and eager.

"Condom," Alex finally said, somewhere between a grunt and a sob.

Damian reached back into the drawer, the movement driving his fingers ever deeper into Alex, who cursed up a blue streak, his cock dripping pre-cum onto his stomach and his face contorted with pleasure.

It was awkward gripping the condom wrapper with his left hand while he opened it very carefully with his teeth, but Damian was reluctant to disconnect from Alex until it was absolutely necessary. He managed to roll the condom on, but had to pause for a moment and squeeze the base of his cock when just that simple caress threatened to send him over the edge.

He didn't need to ask Alex if he was ready — Alex was lifting his hips off the pillow in silent entreaty, and, when Damian slipped his fingers free of his body, Alex muttered a plaintive protest. Damian got on all fours over his lover and opened Alex's mouth with his tongue while he guided his painfully hard cock into him.

As Damian slid home, inch by inch, until he was in Alex to the hilt, Alex breathed in shallow pants into

Damian's mouth and clutched at his biceps. A quick glance at his lover's face reassured Damian that there was no pain. He pulled out a little and eased back in, and a groan rumbled up from his chest at the sensations that zinged along some invisible connection from his crotch to his brain.

"Ah, Jesus Christ!" Damian lowered his body so that he was pressed against Alex from sternum to pelvis. He moved his hips in a circular motion, grinding against Alex, wishing it were possible to get even deeper inside him.

"Fuck, yes." Alex brought his hands down to grab on to Damian's arse and dug his fingers in as though he wanted the very same thing. "Move, Damian, please."

They were damp with sweat, sliding against each other, fingers slipping where they tried to grip. In an attempt to gain better leverage, Damian brought his knees up tighter under his body and lifted Alex's leg to hook it over his shoulder. When he withdrew almost all the way and pushed back in they both cried out in unison, the elation rushing through Damian mirrored in Alex's blissed-out expression.

Higher brain function ceased then, and base need took over. Damian thrust mindlessly, seeking more of Alex's tight heat, more pleasure, reaching for the release that was just beyond his grasp.

Alex rose to meet every pounding snap of Damian's hips, begging, cursing. Cries and demands bounced off the walls and the combined scents of sweat and sex filled the air.

"Can't...hold on." Damian worked a hand between their bodies and wrapped his fingers around Alex's prick, squeezing and stroking in time to his increasingly erratic thrusts. Alex howled his delight and his hole rippled around Damian's cock. Damian's hips stuttered, heat gathered at the base of his spine and he rammed into Alex one more time, arching his back and coming so hard that flashes of colour exploded behind his eyelids.

"Holy *fuck*!" Alex dug his nails into Damian's arse and stopped breathing altogether as his cock pulsed warm and wet between their bodies.

Out of breath and suddenly weak as a kitten, Damian collapsed, sliding to rest beside Alex, dragging in great gulps of air.

Alex turned on to his side, one leg draped over Damian's hip, and pushed the damp hair from Damian's forehead. "That was fucking amazing."

A lazy smile tugged at Damian's mouth. "Oh, yeah, we're definitely doing that again." He laid his hand on Alex's thigh and stroked his thumb back and forth — all the exertion he had the energy for at that moment.

They were quiet for a long time, pressed close together as their bodies cooled.

"What does it feel like?" Damian finally asked.

Alex stopped nuzzling into Damian's neck and lifted his head. "Having you inside me?"

Pleased that Alex knew what he was asking, Damian nodded and turned his head on the pillow to meet his lover's eyes.

"Physically, I felt full, stretched to the limit. Every time you pushed into me I wanted to open up a little further, take you in a little deeper. I could feel your cock stroking every nerve-ending, and when you hit my prostate I thought the top of my head was going to blow off." He laughed softly and ran his thumb over Damian's bottom lip. "Emotionally, I just felt whole for the first time in my life."

Damian took Alex's hand and touched the tip of his tongue to the pad of Alex's thumb. He wanted to wrap himself around Alex completely, to absorb the warmth and generosity and kindness, and everything that made him *Alex*. "I want to do it; I want to take you inside my body."

All the air seemed to leave Alex's lungs in a loud rush. "God, Damian, I can't even begin to tell you how much I want that. When the time's right." He leaned in and brushed his lips against Damian's in a whisper-soft kiss.

Damian sighed into the kiss, inhaled Alex's scent and marvelled at the sense of peace it brought with it.

Chapter Seventeen

"It's Monday," Damian said, his voice muffled by the pillow.

Alex smiled, turned towards his lover, and wrapped an arm around Damian's waist under the sheet they'd pulled over themselves last night. "Stunning observation, Sherlock."

"Smart arse." Damian pinched Alex's rear. "I meant that it's Monday and I don't have to be up at the arse crack of dawn to go to work. I can't remember the last time I didn't have somewhere to be on a Monday morning."

"Hmm, yeah, I know what you mean; I've been thinking the same thing for a couple of weeks now. I think it's time we both started looking for jobs." In spite of his words, Alex made no attempt to move beyond smoothing a hand up and down Damian's back. There was really nowhere else he wanted to be.

"Shit, I've never had to look for work before," Damian sounded more amused than disturbed. "I walked out of uni and into an executive position at Stanhope Developments. Do people still use CVs?"

Alex tucked his head into the place where Damian's neck and shoulder met and snickered. "Poor little rich boy."

"Fuck you," Damian muttered. He slipped a leg between Alex's and rubbed his thigh against Alex's stirring cock.

Alex sighed and pushed closer. "Mm, yes, that would be a lovely way to start the day."

"Unfortunately, I have to piss." Damian moved suddenly, rolled Alex on to his back and leaned over him. With a wide, teasing smile, he dropped a brief, almost chaste kiss on Alex's lips and got out of bed.

"You're such a fucking romantic, Stanhope." Alex laughed and turned on to his side to watch Damian walk across the room to the bathroom. The pull and release of muscle under smooth skin was mesmerising, and Alex was certain Damian was putting an extra little swing into his hips, just for him. "I'll make coffee and we can talk about what you're going to do with your useless arse."

"Nothing useless about this arse, Jennings." Damian glanced over his shoulder and winked. "You'll see."

Sensation shivered through Alex. *Can't wait.*

Dressed in yesterday's boxers, Alex left the bedroom, which was sectioned off from the main area by a frosted glass screen, and headed for the kitchen area at the far end of the vast room. He was standing and staring at a huge stainless steel coffee machine, with more knobs and buttons than a space shuttle, when he heard Damian's soft footsteps approaching. "Are you serious with this thing?"

Damian grinned and nudged Alex out of the way, then set about making the coffee with impressive ease and dexterity. When he turned back to Alex and handed him a cup of steaming, aromatic espresso, he looked so pleased with himself that Alex's heart squeezed in his chest.

"God, that's good," Alex said after taking a sip. "Well, I'd say that's one problem solved." Damian frowned, clearly puzzled, and Alex leaned in to kiss the tip of his nose. "With skills like that you could easily get a job in Starbucks. Hell, you'd be head barista in a week."

Damian shook his head, trying unsuccessfully to look wounded. "You have a gorgeous, naked man making you delicious coffee and you're making bad jokes? I may have to rethink the whole moving in together thing."

"Aw, babe." Alex set his cup down on the granite worktop and placed his hands on Damian's hips, easing him back against the island in the middle of the kitchen. "You don't mean that. How can I make it up to you?" He angled his head to nibble on Damian's earlobe and was gratified to feel the shift of Damian's cock against his hip.

"Did you call me babe?" Damian slipped a hand down the back of Alex's shorts and cupped a cheek.

Alex lifted his head, one eyebrow arched. "You don't like?"

For a second Damian seemed to seriously consider it, and then his smile widened. "I like."

Warmth radiated out from Alex's chest and he nodded. "Okay, then." He wrapped one arm around Damian's waist, lifted the other to sift his fingers through Damian's bed-mussed hair and pulled him into a kiss. Damian wound his arms around Alex's shoulders and opened his mouth to deepen the kiss. It went from hot to scorching in a split second. They strained against each other, tongues sweeping together, breathing hard.

The sound of tinny music gradually pierced the veil of arousal dimming any senses not completely immersed in the kiss. Alex pulled back reluctantly, blinking to clear his fuzzy vision. "What...?"

Damian sighed and rested his forehead against Alex's. "Imogen. I was supposed to call her yesterday to let her know what happened."

It took a moment, but the tune playing on the phone finally registered with Alex and he laughed. "Oh my God, does Imogen know her assigned ringtone is The Eagles' *Witchy Woman*?"

Damian snorted. "Of course not. Do you think I'd be standing here in one piece if she did?"

"She's just going to keep calling if you don't answer, isn't she?" Alex guessed.

"She might even come over. The woman is nosier than a room full of cats." There was fondness in Damian's tone. "We could try to ignore her, but, unfortunately, I gave her a key for emergencies. I doubt she'd have any hesitation in using it."

The phone went silent and they both waited, barely breathing. When the song started over again less than a minute later, laughter bubbled up and they leaned against each other.

"I should answer," Damian said, "If I don't I'll have to get dressed just in case she comes over, because she no longer has the privilege of seeing me in all my glory. Besides, I need to ask her for that key back. It has a new owner now."

Alex chuckled and slapped Damian's rear when he turned away to pick up the phone, and a thought occurred to him. "Hey, what's my ringtone?"

Dots of embarrassed colour touched Damian's cheekbones and he shrugged. "The, uh, the theme from *Doctor Who*."

When Alex convulsed with laughter, Damian gave him the finger and turned away to answer the phone. Alex picked up his coffee and crossed the room to the wall of windows, then opened one enough to step out on to the balcony. It was only just after seven in the morning and the air was a little cool, but there was a haze hanging over the city, so Alex was pretty sure it was going to be a lovely day. He leaned on the railing and sipped his coffee while he looked around him. The Thames was still quite quiet at that time, with only the occasional water bus or river police boat gliding by. In the distance he could see the dome of St Paul's Cathedral and the City of London, probably gearing up for another day of trying to keep a step ahead of the recession.

A tap on the window caught his attention and he turned around to find Damian standing on the other side of the glass, a private smile playing around his lips and crooking his finger in a 'Come hither' manner. Alex laughed softly, put his cup down on a low, teak table set between two matching chairs and went back inside. When he was within reach, Damian took both of his hands and walked backwards in the direction of the bedroom.

* * * *

"Oh my God, oh my God!" Imogen pulled first Damian then Alex into tight hugs, high-pitched, incomprehensible babble spilling from her lips, heedless of the looks she was receiving from the other diners in the restaurant. "I'm so happy for you both."

Damian pulled out a chair at their table and coaxed Imogen into it before taking the seat next to Alex. They were on the terrace, overlooking Covent Garden, the sounds of the market below drifting to them on a summer-scented breeze. Alex laced his fingers with Damian's when his lover laid a hand over his.

"Thanks, sweetheart, and I'm sorry I didn't phone yesterday; it was all a bit frantic." Damian's fingers tightened on Alex's where they rested on Alex's thigh, and Alex smoothed his thumb over Damian's knuckles. He was no longer feeling guilty per se, but, every time he thought of the rift between Damian and his father, a knot of remorse formed in his chest.

"You told Grayson?" Imogen asked, her eyes wide and curious. To Alex she looked more like a gossipy schoolgirl than the sophisticated magazine editor she was.

"He worked it out on his own. He wasn't thrilled." Damian shrugged carelessly, but Alex knew he wasn't as unaffected as he sought to appear. The knot twisted.

A waiter arrived then to take their drinks orders, and, when he left, Alex tried to change the subject by asking Imogen how her work was going, but, aside from a brief update, she was clearly more interested in finding out every little detail she could about the debacle at Garnet House the day before. Like a dog with a bone — or a journalist with a lead — she refused to let go until Damian capitulated and answered her questions.

They ordered their food when the waiter returned with a bottle of white wine and three glasses, and Alex was thankful when Imogen — one appetite apparently satisfied, for the moment at least — turned her attention to her seafood salad. Damian turned to Alex and rolled his eyes, smiling, obviously used to Imogen's ways and therefore unfazed by her single-minded focus.

The rest of lunch passed pleasantly with the talk turning to more neutral topics that eased the acid rising in Alex's stomach and made it easier to eat his herb omelette. When Imogen excused herself, with a flurry of kisses and promises to catch up soon, to return to work, Alex and Damian relaxed in the shade of the covered terrace and finished the bottle of wine, hands once more touching under the table, instinctively leaning towards each other as they spoke quietly, as if they had a bubble around them that excluded the rest of the world.

When they left the restaurant they drove to Alex's parents' house in Wimbledon, where they found Robert in the middle of setting up a large-screen TV and home cinema system in the living room, and Beth, having given up on the idea of a goat because she'd been chased by one at the city farm and had *'barely made it out alive'*, was in the kitchen with the plans for a very elaborate rabbit hutch spread out on the table.

Alex laughed, even as he winced, at his mother's shriek of delight when he and Damian told them their news, and his dad pulled Damian into a crushing hug, thumping him on the back with enough enthusiasm to leave Damian breathless and bug-eyed. Beth offered to open a bottle of her homemade elderflower wine in celebration, but Alex, having sampled the bitter brew and being reluctant to subject his taste buds to it a second time, opted for orange juice since he was driving. He watched, amusement simmering, as Damian took a sip of the wine and an expression of horror flashed across his face before he managed to conceal it and nodded his approval to Beth.

"So, uh, Robert, would you like some help with that home cinema system? I set up my own a while back," Damian asked eagerly, putting his glass down on the table. When his dad accepted the offer just as enthusiastically, Alex chuckled at the relief that brightened Damian's eyes. He followed Robert through to the living room, leaving his near-full glass where it was.

"Oh, darling, I'm so pleased for you." Beth lifted her hands to cup Alex's face, her eyes shining with emotion. "He's... Well, I couldn't have wished for more for you."

"Yeah, he'll do, I suppose." Alex grinned. "I need to pack up my things and get the key to my storage unit."

Beth feigned shock, her hands moving to clasp over her chest. "You're going to be living in sin? What will the neighbours think?"

Laughing, Alex dropped a kiss on Beth's forehead. "If you weren't growing pot in the greenhouse, I might take you seriously." He dodged the swat Beth aimed at him and took the stairs two at a time.

When he'd left for Africa, Alex had sold his flat and most of his furniture, and put the rest of his belongings into a storage locker. When he'd returned, with nothing but the clothes on his back, he'd been forced to buy a few things. That his parents had a computer and a high-speed broadband connection was a godsend, meaning that he hadn't had to leave the house at a time when he was going through the worst of the nightmares and flashbacks. As a result, he didn't have much more to pack, beyond the things already at Damian's. Ten minutes later he was back downstairs, standing in the living room doorway with the bag at his feet.

Damian had his sleeves rolled up and was up to his elbows in wires and cables, eyebrows pulled together in concentration. As Alex watched, Damian's head shot up like a dog that had caught a scent and he turned, his eyes meeting Alex's. Damian smiled softly and Alex just about melted. *Jesus, I've got it bad.* He felt the bag resting against his foot and it really hit him for the first time. This was actually happening. He was going to live with Damian, make a life with him.

A mixture of exhilaration and terror seethed in Alex. It was rather a frightening thing, he found, to have a dream come true.

Chapter Eighteen

"I've been looking online for stables for Apollo and I've found a few not far away. Do you want to come with me and check them out?" Damian was stretched out on the bed, propped up on a stack of pillows with his laptop balanced on his knees.

Alex turned from the bookcase where he was trying to find room on the shelves for the books he'd got out of storage. For a week now, he and Damian had been working, mostly side by side, to blend their belongings. Alex's toothbrush now sat next to Damian's in the bathroom, their CDs, DVDs and Blu-rays were mixed together in the entertainment console, and the wall adjacent to the nude in the dining area was now hung with a collection of pictures Alex had taken.

"Sure. Actually, I was thinking about getting a horse of my own. I enjoyed riding with you at the estate." Alex turned back to the bookcase, but not before Damian saw the flicker of emotion that crossed his face.

Damian suppressed a sigh. It was going to take a while to convince Alex that he was not to blame for the problems between Damian and Grayson. A part of him wanted to shake the man and demand that he *listen, damn it*, but the rest of him—the greater part—was just so gone on Alex that everything he did was fucking adorable. He grinned. "Yeah, I've discovered that riding with you is one of my favourite things to do."

"I can't believe you said that; you're such a twat." Alex didn't turn around, but Damian could hear the amusement in his voice and it heartened him. "You have two copies of *The Hobbit* and I have one. Charity pile?" He held up the two extra copies.

The charity pile had been growing daily, making them both realise just how similar their tastes in music, movies and books were. "I think I also have two copies of that Vonnegut novel, *Slaughterhouse-Five*. Chuck them on the pile."

"Both of them?" Alex asked as he looked over his shoulder, an eyebrow cocked in question.

Damian shrugged. "I tried. It didn't take."

The books landed on the floor with twin muffled thumps. "I don't think there's going to be enough room. Can you clear some space in the cupboard?"

"No problem." Damian was about to set the laptop aside when he heard the ping that announced the arrival of an email. He clicked on the tab and his smile widened when he saw that it was from Romilly. They'd been receiving almost daily updates from his sister on her family holiday, usually with photos or short videos attached. "Hey, Alex, there's a new video clip from Romilly."

Alex came to the bed and climbed up beside Damian. His hair was still slightly damp from the shower, and the smell of shampoo and soap drifted to Damian. He found himself leaning closer to Alex, nuzzling into his temple. Alex smiled and twisted his neck to press a kiss to Damian's lips. "Email," he reminded, his voice muffled against Damian's mouth when Damian started to press him back against the pillows.

Apart from Alex signing on with an agency just the day before to do some locum work while he looked for a permanent job, their talk of finding work had fallen victim to long, lazy days of indulging in long lie-ins, making love, slow and easy, with rays of sun pouring through the windows, or heated and energetic, with a glittering, night-time London as their backdrop. When they'd ventured out it had been to one of the many local pubs or restaurants, lingering over good food and fine wine, oblivious to anything beyond each other. Damian's only complaint, minor as it was, was that Alex had held on to his concerns that Damian might not yet be ready to bottom for him. As much as he loved the man for caring, Damian intended to put him right on that front very soon.

"Email," Damian said and dropped another light kiss on Alex's mouth before settling back against the pillows, one arm around Alex's shoulders to coax him nearer. While the video downloaded, Damian read the text aloud.

Hi Guys,
Another gorgeous day here on the English Riviera. Michael and I took Belle to the bird sanctuary yesterday. Some of the rarest birds in the world; she was thoroughly unimpressed (see vid.). Susan and Hugh are taking her to the model village today (expect pics of 'giant' marauding

baby), so Michael and I are hiring a boat and plan on making whoopee on the waves!

I daresay you two are giving the bedsprings (and the tables, worktops, shower, etc. etc.) a good old workout. Please — no pics or videos!

Love you both,

Romilly, Michael and Belle.

They both laughed, and when Damian hit the button to play the video the laughter increased. Michael and Romilly were trying to get Belle to look at the penguins, Michael behind the camera making silly noises while Romilly mimicked the birds' movements. Belle, however, was far more interested in playing with her toes while she blew pretty impressive spit bubbles.

"She really is a little beauty," Alex said, voicing Damian's thoughts.

The video only lasted just over a minute. They watched it again before setting the laptop aside, fond smiles lingering as they headed for the walk-in cupboard Damian used for storage.

"Oh my God, you're a pack rat." Alex looked around him at the boxes stacked six high and three deep all around the cupboard. Each box was identical in shape and size, with a small label identifying the contents on the upper right corner. Alex snickered. "An anally retentive pack rat. Why weren't you this neat when we shared at uni?"

Damian nudged Alex aside with his shoulder and a scowl he wasn't feeling. "This is a lifetime of memories and treasured mementos."

"I don't know; my little box might feel overwhelmed and inferior in here." Alex flicked at a torn cardboard flap, trying to look forlorn, but not quite pulling it off as humour sparkled in his eyes.

"Dick," Damian said, stifling a laugh. He looked around for a space to tuck Alex's box into, and saw a box marked 'Proposals'. "Here, I'll move this one; it can go in the office."

"You kept a record of your proposals? Couldn't you just recycle the same one over and over again? It's not like the wives were going to compare notes." Alex slipped his box onto the shelf, patting it as if to reassure it.

"*Business* proposals; and you call *me* a twat." Shaking his head and laughing softly, Damian carried the box through to the office and set it down on the glass-topped desk. Out of curiosity, he removed the lid and his eyes widened. "Well, damn."

"What is it? Did you find those plans for world domination?" Alex came to stand beside him and Damian bumped him with a hip in lieu of an insult.

"No, just something I wasted six months of my life on." He removed one of the folders and glanced over the sheets of laboriously calculated costings and projections, knowing that the other folders contained lists of suppliers, construction contractors, architects and designers, and photographs of unique and unusual buildings. He felt a stab of remembered pain and his hand tightened on the papers, threatening to crush them. "A few years ago I had this idea. I wanted Stanhope to move into boutique hotels. We've always catered to the super-rich, who expect and get first class service; the best of everything. I wanted to offer a little of that to middle-income people. People shouldn't have to be listed in *Who's Who?* to be treated special. The big chain hotels are fine — most of them give good service and value for money, but boutique hotels offer a more personalised experience where the rooms are individually designed and the focus is on customer service at an affordable rate." Damian sighed and dropped the file back in the box.

"But?" Alex asked, hand on Damian's back, encouraging.

Damian shrugged as if it was nothing, but he could still feel the sharp disappointment of his father's dismissal. "Grayson told me to stop wasting my damn time and get back to the job I was being paid for. He said boutique hotels were too low-rent to be bothered with; beneath a company of our standing and reputation." Replacing the lid, Damian slid the box under the desk to be dealt with later. When he turned to Alex, he could see annoyance in his eyes and he was biting his lip as if holding something back. Damian's smile wouldn't be contained. "Come on, out with it."

After a slight pause, Alex gritted out. "With all due respect, your father is a bloody fool."

Damian got the feeling that was the sanitised version of what Alex was thinking, but it warmed him nonetheless. He lifted a hand and trailed the backs of his fingers down Alex's cheek. "No argument here, love. Why don't we just forget about him and get out for a while? I want to get Apollo moved as soon as possible, so the sooner we find a stable for him, the better."

"Okay. I'll just go and get changed." With a frown still creasing his forehead, Alex placed a featherlight kiss on Damian's palm and turned towards the bedroom.

* * * *

There were four stables on Damian's list, two in Bexley, one in Kingston upon Thames and one in Epsom. Since it was a bright, sunny day, they took Damian's black Mercedes and put the top down to make the most of the cooling breeze. They drove to Bexley, where he immediately ruled out the first stable for being too close to the residential area and not having enough grassland. The second in Bexley was a definite possibility — the staff were well trained, the loose boxes clean and well maintained, and there was plenty of space for Apollo to run. Kingston upon Thames, though nicely kept, seemed more geared towards teaching, with their clientele being mostly children.

They stopped for a bite to eat at a cafe on the river before continuing on to Epsom. The minute he laid eyes on Hollister Farm Stables, Damian knew he'd found Apollo's new home. Set in nearly a hundred acres of land, there were several lush green fields bordered by woodland and a horseshoe-shaped courtyard surrounded by solid, clean loose boxes. The owner, Harriet Baker — a middle-aged woman with a no-nonsense attitude, sharp grey eyes and cropped salt and pepper hair — answered all of Damian's questions without hesitation, gave him the name of the vet they used so that he could check the man out, as well as a sheaf of testimonials, and introduced him to the owners present that day. She showed him everything from the food stores to the tack room and the all-weather exercise arena. But it was the way her eyes softened when she spoke to the horses that sold Damian on the place.

By the time they left, Damian was smiling like a fool and Alex was looking through a brochure of horses entrusted to Harriet for sale.

It was late evening when they arrived home, having stopped off at the supermarket to pick up some food and wine, and to replenish their rapidly dwindling stock of lube and condoms. Damian had definite plans for those in the night ahead, but first he wanted to soften Alex up so that his lover would be amenable to them.

"Why don't you go and freshen up and I'll put on a couple of steaks. We can eat on the balcony and open a bottle of that burgundy you like?" Damian dumped the shopping bags on the kitchen island and reached for a bottle opener.

"Sounds good. I'll just check the machine in case the agency called when we were out." Alex crossed to the office and hit the button on the answering machine, but, instead of someone from the employment agency, it was Martha's voice that drifted to Damian.

"Damian, could, uh, could you call me when you get in. Please…it – it's important, dear."

Unease turned over in Damian's gut. He set the open bottle on the worktop and went to the phone. Alex remained beside him while he dialled, his face reflecting his own concern.

Martha answered on the second ring, and started speaking as soon as she'd confirmed it was Damian on the other end, her voice shaky and uneven. Damian listened with a growing sense of disconnection from reality, nodding even though he knew Martha couldn't see him. He began to quake and his knees felt weak, like they were about to give out on him at any second. "Yes, yes, I understand. Goodbye, Ma," he finally said, though it was barely audible and he didn't recognise the sound of his own voice. When he replaced the receiver and turned to Alex, Damian's vision was so hazy he had to lift his hand and touch him to reassure himself that Alex was really there.

"Damian, talk to me." Alex put his hands under Damian's elbows and guided him to the chair behind the desk.

Damian sat, hands gripping Alex's biceps. Martha's words echoed in his head. "There was an accident. Romilly and Michael, their boat... Alex?"

"I'm right here, love." Alex crouched in front of him and Damian blinked to bring him into focus.

"They're dead, Alex. Romilly and Michael... They're dead." Was that his voice? Had he just said that?

Chapter Nineteen

Romilly and Michael were to be buried side by side in the Stanhope family vault. Grayson arranged for the transport of the bodies from Devon to Garnet House, sent a car to bring Susan, Hugh and Belle to the estate, and organised the funeral service, all within four days of the accident. All without once contacting Damian. Alex swore vehemently that he would never forgive Grayson for that slight. It was petty, unnecessary and downright cruel.

The official accident report was that two young men — still in their late teens and on holiday without parental supervision for the first time — had been messing about on a small cabin cruiser they'd taken from the harbour without the owner's knowledge or permission. They had still been drunk from the night before and unaware that the boat was about to undergo repairs for a leak in the fuel line. They had crashed into Romilly and Michael's hired boat. The resultant explosion was seen for miles and there had been no survivors. Four families devastated in one horrible moment.

Martha had been calling at least once a day to keep Damian and Alex in the loop — Alex had no doubt that she was doing it of her own volition, with no instruction from Grayson.

Two weeks to the day since Alex had arrived at Garnet House for the weekend, he and Damian returned, a cloud of grief hanging heavy over them. They hadn't been officially invited, but Alex was prepared to take the damn place by storm if Grayson tried to stop Damian from saying this final goodbye to his baby sister.

Damian had been unnaturally quiet since Martha's first phone call, his eyes hollow from too little sleep, his skin so pale that the dusting of freckles over his nose, acquired during their day out looking at stables, stood out in stark relief. He hadn't kept Alex at a distance, though; far from it. When they lay in bed together at night Damian all but wrapped himself around Alex until their bodies were sticky from the heat and contact. He sat so close to Alex on the sofa that he might as well have crawled into Alex's lap. When they left the apartment to buy some groceries or collect suits from the dry cleaners, Damian held Alex's hand every step of the way, his grip almost painful, heedless of the looks they got on the street.

It was like he needed the unbroken connection to stay grounded, to keep him from drifting away.

"Ready?" Alex asked when they got out of the Mercedes in front of Garnet House. He held out his hand as Damian came around the car and latched on to it like a lifeline.

"I don't think I'll ever be ready for this, but... Okay, yes, I'm okay." He attempted a smile and it broke Alex's heart. Damian had yet to shed a tear, and Alex was terrified that, when he did, the grief might be so overwhelming it could shatter Damian, and Alex might not be able to hold him together.

Alex tamped down his fears. This was not about him. He had to be strong for Damian, no matter what. It was a cruel irony that, in trying to focus on Damian's needs, Alex's own demons had faded into the background. He hadn't had a single dream about Africa all week.

Hand in hand, they climbed the stairs to the front door, but, before they could knock, it opened and Helen was there, stoic as ever, but with deep lines of sadness bracketing her mouth and eyes. "Damian, oh my dear boy, I'm so very sorry." Not demonstrative by nature, it was something of a surprise to see Helen envelope Damian in her arms, clearly fighting back the tears that shone in her eyes.

Damian, never letting go of Alex's hand, smoothed his other hand over Helen's back. "Thank you, Helen. Romilly was very fond of you, I hope you know that."

A tear swelled and dripped on to her lower lashes and Helen hastily swiped it away. "She was a very special girl. Come on. Let's get you boys out of this sun before you melt in those suits." She ushered them into the cool hallway.

"Where's Pa?" Damian asked. For the last four days, his voice, when he'd spoken, had been whisper soft, but there was a hard edge to it when he mentioned his father.

Helen gestured to the drawing room door. "They're in there." She turned to leave, but stopped beside Alex and said quietly, "You're taking care of him?"

"Nothing else matters," Alex replied, hoping she heard the truth in his words and tone.

With a brief nod and a soft smile, Helen left them.

When Damian opened the door and he and Alex stepped into the drawing room, the head of every occupant turned in their direction. Though he was aware of the presence of Naomi, Will and Felicity, and, of course, Michael's parents, Susan and Hugh, Alex's gaze was drawn directly to Grayson. The man was standing to one side of the grand stone fireplace, hands clasped behind his back and a dark scowl on his face as he determinedly did not look at Damian. If he hadn't been so fucking angry with him, Alex would have laughed at the image Grayson presented—the great patriarch, master of all he surveyed. But he wasn't. He wasn't the master of his son; and the knowledge galled him so much that he couldn't set it aside, even now. Foolish, small man. Alex turned away, resolved to give Grayson Stanhope no more of his emotional energy. That was reserved solely for Damian.

Susan moved then, breaking the frozen atmosphere in the room. She came to Damian and pulled him into a tight hug. She was a small woman, her dark hair just brushing Damian's chin, her brown eyes filled with more anguish than any mother should have to endure. Damian hugged back, one-armed, but they said nothing as they held on to each other. What words could there be at such a time? When Susan dropped one of her arms and curled her fingers around Alex and Damian's joined hands before stepping away to rejoin her husband, Alex imagined he could actually feel the woman's pain and a surge of grief rose in him so that he had to swallow and blink away the threatening tears.

"Damian, I'm so damn sorry," Will said, coming to stand beside them. He laid a hand on Alex's shoulder and gripped Damian's arm. Alex could tell from the tightness around his mouth that Will was fighting to retain his own composure.

Damian nodded, laying a hand on his cousin's arm. "Thanks, Will." Alex's gaze followed Damian's when he looked over Will's shoulder at Naomi and Felicity. Neither woman met his eyes; they glanced at Grayson before lowering their heads, clearly uncomfortable. Alex wanted to give them a shake. What the hell was this, the nineteenth century? Did they need that bastard's approval to think and speak, too?

Seated beside his wife, the handles of his wheelchair just visible beside the sofa, Hugh looked defeated, as if unaware of where he even was. His face was pale and gaunt, his blue eyes tortured. Alex ached for him. How did a man deal with the death of his only son?

Alex felt a sudden and unexpected stab of sympathy for Grayson. He'd lost his daughter, his youngest child. It had to be tearing his heart out. Dear God, how was it possible to feel genuine sorrow and loathing for one man at the same time?

"Where's Belle?" Damian asked, directing the question at Susan.

"She's upstairs asleep, Helen has been keeping an eye on her." Susan's face seemed to crumple and she took a deep, restorative breath, but when she spoke again her voice was shaky. "I don't think we should take her to the funeral. Do you think we should take her, Damian?"

Alex actually heard Damian swallow and he squeezed Damian's hand. "I think we should let her sleep, Susan. She'll be safe with Helen."

They turned when there was a quiet knock at the door and Helen entered. "Mr Stanhope, Reverend Trace is here to begin the service."

"Thank you, Helen, we'll be right there." Grayson held out his arm to Naomi and started towards the door, followed by Susan and Hugh, with Will pushing Hugh's chair and Felicity linking her arm through Susan's.

As he passed Damian, Grayson finally looked at his son, and for a moment it appeared that he wanted to say something, but instead he lowered his gaze and left the room. Hugh reached out and touched Damian's hand on his way past, a simple show of empathy and acceptance.

Alex and Damian fell in behind the small procession and they were led outside into the sunshine by the solemn, stick-like figure of Reverend Trace. It was to be a private, family service, they'd been told, with a memorial service to be held at a later date for Romilly and Michael's friends.

The vault, in a tranquil glade behind the house, was a simple, elegant structure of Portland stone with an intricate wrought iron fence around it. Romilly and Michael had been placed in the vault the evening before by the undertaker, in preparation for the funeral.

The last time Alex had stood at the vault when the door had been open had been at Damian's mother's funeral ten years before. Damian had cried then, tears glistening on his cheeks while soft, almost inaudible sobs escaped him. Today he was still and silent, eyes focused straight ahead, mouth pulled down at the corners. In spite of the raw emotion around them, sadness so thick and heavy it was almost palpable, Damian's façade showed no signs of cracking. A part of Alex had hoped the funeral would help Damian to let go. As much as he hated the thought of his lover in pain, Alex knew that this limbo Damian was caught in was so much worse. If he didn't allow himself to grieve he would never heal.

The Reverend Trace had a thin, reedy voice that scored the air like nails on a blackboard. Fortunately, unlike others in his profession, he was not a man inclined to ramble, so the service was fairly short. Alex recalled how distressed a fourteen-year-old Romilly had been at her mother's funeral, a service that had lasted for almost two hours with maudlin music and person after person stepping up to speak of their memories of Lavinia and what she'd meant to them, each one more upset than the last. In the end Romilly had had to be led away, nearly hysterical. Alex thought she would have appreciated the brevity of her own send-off.

A sound to his left caught Alex's attention. When he turned he saw Grayson. The man's shoulders were shaking, he had a white-knuckled grip on Naomi's hand, and one look at his face told Alex that Grayson was barely holding it together. Alex understood the reason for the simple, short ceremony—Grayson was afraid of breaking down in front of an audience, even his own family. Alex wasn't sure what he pitied most about Grayson right then—the pain he was clearly feeling at the loss of his daughter, or the fact that he was so tightly wound he couldn't even let his closest loved ones see that pain.

When the Reverend closed his book with a quiet finality, two sombrely dressed men Alex hadn't noticed before—employees of the funeral director, he assumed—stepped forward and closed the doors to the vault. Damian jerked at the sound of the heavy doors shutting and his eyes widened, looking heavenward. Alex moved to stand in front of him, and brought his free hand up to rest on Damian's chest, over his heart. Damian attempted a smile, but he looked weary, tired to his bones.

"Will you come back to the house, Damian, Alex?" Susan asked, touching Alex's shoulder. "The, uh, the solicitor will be here soon to…read the will."

Damian nodded his assent and Alex smiled, though what he really wanted was to get Damian away from this place as soon as possible.

While they were gone, Martha had laid out tea, coffee and a few platters of sandwiches in the drawing room. Felicity poured the tea, but no one made any move towards the food. Grayson returned to stand by the fireplace, but this time with his back to the room. Naomi sat in the chair nearest to him, casting concerned looks in her husband's direction, and Will headed for the decanters set out on a refectory table. He poured scotch into two glasses, took a long sip from one and pressed the other into Hugh's hand.

Alex and Damian sat together on the window seat. They refused Felicity's offer of tea or coffee, but Alex tilted his head to Will in a silent request and the man brought another crystal glass of scotch to Damian.

"I need to go and see Martha before we leave," Damian said quietly, setting the glass down, untouched.

Alex nodded. "Hey, do you think she'd let you get away without a hug? She'd chase us down with that wooden spoon of hers."

"She *is* lethal with that thing." A small huff of laughter escaped Damian and he leaned closer to Alex. "Damn, it's always so fucking cold in this room."

The room was far from cold; cooler than outside, certainly, but they were sitting with their backs to the window with the sun hitting them through the glass.

If anything, Alex felt a little warm. He took both of Damian's hands in his and rubbed them; they did feel a bit cold. He was going to have to watch Damian for the signs of shock.

The door opened then, and Helen appeared again. "Mr Weatherby is here, sir."

Alex's guess that this was the solicitor was confirmed when the man, as wide as he was tall, with thinning grey hair and an expensive suit that looked like it had been cut for a man twenty pounds lighter, opened a shiny leather briefcase and removed a slim envelope.

"Ladies and gentlemen, please accept my most sincere condolences on your terrible loss. Mr and Mrs Darcy — Michael and Romilly — visited me shortly after the birth of their daughter Annabelle, keen to ensure she was taken care of should they pass before she reached the age of majority." Weatherby's brow creased as he opened the envelope and withdrew the contents. "Their instructions were very simple. Aside from a few small bequests to family members, friends and charities, the money in their bank accounts and investment portfolio is to be placed into trust for Annabelle. The house in St John's Wood, London, as well as the business, Concept Public Relations, is to be sold and the proceeds placed into the trust fund. It was Mr and Mrs Darcy's greatest wish that Mrs Darcy's brother, Damian Stanhope, should assume guardianship of Annabelle, and administer the trust fund until she reaches the age of twenty-one."

Alex gasped his surprise and turned to Damian just as a single tear spilled over and rolled down his lover's pale cheek.

Chapter Twenty

A kind of numbness had settled on Damian when Martha had called with news of the accident, and for the next four days he'd moved through life as if wrapped in cotton wool, everything muffled and distant, senses dulled, two steps removed from everything and everyone around him. Except Alex. Alex had been his one link to a world that seemed to be slipping further and further away by the hour, and Damian had held on tight. It wasn't that he was in denial, exactly—he didn't expect to be told that it was all a terrible mistake, nor did he expect to have a door open or turn a corner and see his baby sister, smiling, whole and alive. He knew from that first phone call that Romilly was gone, that she wasn't coming back. He'd skipped over several of the steps of grieving right to acceptance, and his mind had promptly shut down, as if to protect him from the pain to come.

He also knew that Alex was deeply concerned about him; could see it in every glance, feel it every time Alex held him a little tighter than was comfortable, but he didn't know how to reassure Alex that he was fine, that he would *be* fine, because he didn't know how he felt, and he'd been dreading the day when the emotional paralysis would lift and he'd actually have to deal with what was happening.

It appeared that day had arrived.

The tear tickled his cheek as it rolled down and Damian raised a hand to wipe it away, looking curiously at his fingers when he saw they were wet. Something shifted in his chest, pressed hard and sharp against his heart, like a piece of shrapnel, and the breath he expelled was fractured and uneven. He wanted desperately to get out, to escape the scrutiny of the eyes watching him, find somewhere private and fall apart.

As if he could sense Damian's growing turmoil, Alex slid closer to him on the window seat, until Damian could feel his lover's warmth all down his side, shoulder to thigh. Alex's grip on his hand was so tight that Damian fancied he could feel every callus on his fingers, every line on his palm. It was enough to sustain Damian. At least for now.

"Me? They want me to have Belle?" he asked Weatherby. His voice felt rough, as if from disuse.

"That was Mr and Mrs Darcy's wish." Weatherby nodded.

As the news sank in, Damian silently marvelled at the wonder that was the human mind. He hadn't been ready to deal with Romilly and Michael's deaths, so his consciousness had shielded him from it, placing him in a protective embrace. But now his mind knew that he no longer had the luxury of hiding from the truth. Belle needed him now, and he was of no use to her in a state where he was barely functioning. This was going to fucking hurt, but it was for Belle.

"This is outrageous." Low as it was, Grayson's angry voice filled the otherwise silent room. He glanced briefly at Damian before turning on the solicitor. "This will was made shortly after Belle was born, you say?"

"That's correct." To his credit, Weatherby didn't so much as flinch under the weight of Grayson's glare.

Grayson nodded and pointed to where Damian and Alex were sitting. "Then that changes everything. Romilly and Michael couldn't possibly have known then that Damian was going to lose his damn mind. My daughter would not have wanted her child raised in such a…situation. I'll contest the will." He flicked his hand at Damian and Alex, part anger, part dismissal, and turned his back on them.

Fury rose fast, and acute, in Damian, for the moment taking precedence over every other emotion, and he sprang to his feet. But before he had a chance to get a word out Susan was standing, her gaze fixed on his father.

"No, Grayson. Romilly loved her brother dearly and she was very happy that he'd finally found his way. She also thought very highly of Alex and I'm certain the change in Damian and Alex's relationship would not have induced either her or Michael to make any changes to their will." Susan moved to stand by Grayson and laid a hand gently on his arm. "This is what our children wanted. We have to respect that; it's the last thing we can do for them."

The stiff set of his father's shoulders told Damian that Grayson wanted to disagree, but he was too much of a gentleman to start an argument with a bereaved mother.

"Well, I don't want to intrude, so I'll take my leave now." Weatherby placed the papers back in his briefcase and closed it with a snap. "I'll be in touch with each of the beneficiaries individually in the next few days to complete the necessary paperwork." He nodded to the room in general and left, closing the door softly behind him.

The silence that followed Weatherby's departure was charged with the energy of unspoken words. Damian half expected Grayson to erupt, manners be damned, but instead his father went to the drinks table and splashed whisky into a glass, then threw it back like it was water.

Damian's ire began to recede and he once more became aware of the ache in his heart, the despair that seemed to be swelling to fill his entire body, the emotion constricting his throat and stinging his eyes.

"You wanted to see Martha, why don't we go and do that?" Alex asked, moving to stand beside him, partially concealing him from the others.

Damian nodded, hoping his gratitude showed in his expression. He was starting to tremble now and knew it wouldn't be long until the cracks began to show. He allowed Alex to usher him out of the room and across the hall, but, instead of heading towards the door to the kitchen, Alex guided him into the library and closed the door.

"Was it really only two weeks ago we shared our first kiss in here?" Damian asked. His eyes went to the bookcases and for a minute he saw them there, finally admitting to what had always been between them. His vision blurred, and when he blinked he felt the spill of tears on his cheeks.

Alex was right there, as he had been for the last four days, for the last fifteen years, pulling Damian into his arms, cradling Damian's head against his shoulder while he murmured soft words of comfort. For a heartbeat Damian fought against the oncoming tidal wave, but he was no match for the power of the emotions that ripped through him and he crumpled against Alex, allowing his lover to take his weight; trusting Alex not to let him fall.

The sobs that racked Damian's body were muffled by Alex's shoulder, his tears absorbed by the fabric of Alex's jacket. Damian knew that, if it were possible, Alex would gladly absorb Damian's pain, lift the heavy weight from around Damian's heart and carry it himself. As it was, he held Damian through it all, holding him together when he was certain he would have splintered into a million pieces.

He had no idea how long they stayed that way, but Alex never once tried to rush him or urge him to pull himself together. He kept up a litany of whispered endearments while he smoothed his hand in soothing circles on Damian's back. When the worst of the breakdown subsided, to be replaced by exhaustion and the beginnings of a headache, Damian lifted his head from Alex's shoulder and saw that his lover's own eyes were bright with unshed tears.

Expelling a long, shuddering breath, Damian brought his hand up to cup Alex's cheek. "I don't say it anything like enough, but I love you. I feel so blessed to have you in my life."

"Remember the first time we met?" Alex asked, pressing his cheek into Damian's palm. "I came to see you about the room you were renting out. You'd been out on the lash the night before and were hideously hung over. You threw up on my shoes then smiled so sweetly, apologised, and told me I could have the first month rent free. I knew in that moment that you were going to be important to me. I never guessed that you would quickly become the most important person in my life. I loved you then and I love you now."

Damian sighed and rested his forehead against Alex's. "Even when I look like I've been dragged through a hedge backwards?"

A soft huff of laughter brushed Damian's cheek, and Alex pulled back enough to reach for the handkerchief in his pocket. "Well, you are a little snotty, but that can be fixed." He dabbed at Damian's eyes before wiping his nose, and Damian had to laugh, though it sounded more like a hiccup.

"Why don't we go and see Martha now, before she hunts us down?" Damian asked. He pressed a kiss to Alex's lips before running his fingers through his own hair and straightening his tie, though he knew he probably looked wrecked and a straight tie wasn't going to help much.

Alex smoothed his thumb over Damian's eyebrow. "Lead on, babe."

Martha was sitting at the kitchen table, folding and re-folding a tea towel when they entered, her brow furrowed deeply and so lost in her own thoughts that, when she looked up at their arrival, it took a second or two for recognition to flicker to life in her eyes. When she finally *saw* them she was on her feet in an instant, coming around the table with her arms open wide. "Oh, my boys." She gathered them into a kind of group hug that might have been funny in other circumstances.

"Hello, Ma." Damian placed a kiss on top of Martha's head while Alex rubbed a soothing hand up and down her back. "How're you holding up?"

She shook her head, and tears welled up in her eyes. "It's so awful, so unfair." She lifted a hand and touched the tips of her fingers gently to Damian's cheek, as if she were afraid he might break. "My poor loves. Are you looking after each other?" She turned concerned eyes on Alex.

"Always, Ma, always." Alex smiled reassuringly. "But maybe you can help me coax this one to have something to eat?"

"You haven't been eating?" Clearly horrified by the idea, Martha stepped back and shooed them both over to the table. "No, of course you haven't. I can see that just from looking at you."

Damian cocked an eyebrow at Alex as they took their seats, trying to inject a silent accusation of betrayal into his expression, but he knew he'd failed when Alex simply smiled and shrugged. For the first time in days Damian felt real amusement rise in him. It seemed it wasn't just the grief that had been set free by the cracking of the ice around his heart.

"Now, I know it's summer and not really the weather for soup, but it's just about the best comfort food there is, so I have a big pot of my split pea and lentil here, and some fresh crusty bread," Martha said, taking two deep bowls from the cupboard and carrying them to the range. "I'm going to put a bowl in front of you and you will not leave my table until the last spoonful is gone, understood?"

Alex snickered, but his smile faded when Martha turned to him and gave him one of her *looks*. "And I mean both of you. How are you supposed to take care of him if you aren't looking after yourself?"

It was Damian's turn to smile, and, Jesus, that felt good. He took the spoon Martha handed him and looked down at the huge bowl of soup in front of him. There was no way his appetite was up to the full portion, but he knew if he at least ate some that Martha would let him off. Still, as good as it smelt, his stomach clenched at the thought.

"Wonderful as always, Ma," Alex said, tearing off a chunk of bread and dipping it in the soup. The expression on his face when he put the bread in his mouth was verging on orgasmic. He looked pointedly at Damian then, who, with a sigh of capitulation, lifted a spoonful to his mouth.

Pleasure zinged his taste buds and his stomach rumbled. Perhaps he'd try just a little more. He was aware of the wink Martha sent in Alex's direction, but he pretended he hadn't seen. Let them have their small victory—after all, they were only trying to look after him.

When he put the spoon down a little while later, he was surprised to find that more than half the contents of the bowl were gone, but his attention was quickly diverted by the sound of the door opening, and when he glanced over his shoulder his heart seemed to stutter in his chest.

Before he was even aware of moving, Damian was on his feet, crossing to the door and Helen, her arms filled with a squirming bundle of pink, a fluffy tuft of blonde hair sticking out. He silently held out his arms and Helen placed Belle into them, her hand lingering for a moment on his. Damian smiled at the housekeeper, then turned his gaze to Belle. She was smiling widely, drooling on her fingers, blue eyes bright and curious. She looked so much like Romilly that Damian's heart ached, but he also felt an unexpected stab of joy. Romilly would never be completely gone, not with her daughter's smile to light up their lives.

A tear tracked its way down Damian's cheek, but it held no sting.

Chapter Twenty-One

"Oh, my God, there's so much stuff. How can one tiny little bit of a person need so much stuff?" In the middle of their living room, Damian turned in a slow circle, his stunned gaze taking in the pile of boxes filled with clothes, toys and bedding, the cot, pram, high-chair, changing mat, baby bath, car seat…and on and on it seemed to go. He reached into one of the boxes and withdrew what looked like a twisted roll of fabric. "I don't even know what some of this stuff *is*. I mean, what on earth is *this*?"

Alex chuckled and shifted Belle in his arms in order to put her clutching hands out of the reach of the patch of chest hair visible at the open neck of his shirt. She latched on to his collar instead, dragging it into her mouth with a drool-soaked fist. "It's a baby sling. You use it to carry the baby around and leave your hands free. I've seen women using them in the supermarket."

"Huh. What about this?" He picked up something that looked like it belonged on the international space station and turned it over in his hands, an endearing little frown wrinkling his forehead.

"Bottle steriliser. I believe that one uses steam." Alex carried Belle to the big L-shaped sofa and nestled into the corner with the baby in his lap. He was happy to answer every question Damian could come up with if it stopped the man from dwelling on the emotions that had been dragged back to the surface in the last few days.

Belle had been with them for nearly three weeks now, and until four days ago they'd been making do with the clothes and travel bassinette that Susan and Hugh had brought with them from Devon. Four days ago, however, Damian had decided he was ready to go to Romilly and Michael's house to collect Belle's things, and to start packing up in preparation for the sale. It quickly became clear from Damian's increasing silence, and the way he avoided looking at the many family photos placed around the house, that he wasn't anything like as ready as he said.

Since coming home from the funeral, Damian's mood had lifted daily, thanks in no small part to the presence of Belle, who seemed to work some kind of magic on his bruised soul. Alex had been heartened to see the spark of life return to his lover's eyes, and Damian's laughter, if not as free or effusive as before, still sounded wonderful to Alex's ears.

Visiting Romilly's home, being surrounded by her things, had been a step backwards. Alex knew Damian hadn't slept well since, as tiring as it was looking after a young baby, and even after Alex himself had done his best to exhaust Damian with long, energetic hours of lovemaking after Belle had gone down for the evening. Alex was usually just drifting off himself when he felt the bed beside him shift as Damian grabbed his robe and left their room quietly.

The first night, Alex had followed him and seen Damian walking the floor with Belle sleeping in his arms. Several hours later, and every morning since, Alex had come out of the bedroom to find Damian asleep on the sofa with the baby curled up against his chest.

When they'd discovered that Belle had a lot more than they could fit in the car, they'd arranged to have the boxes delivered; and they'd arrived less than an hour ago. Since then, Damian had been picking through the boxes, examining every bib, stuffed animal and baby blanket the way an archaeologist marvelled over ancient artefacts.

"I think we're going to need to find a bigger place to live," Damian said, sorting through a box of clothing that looked ridiculously tiny in his hands. "Maybe we should look for a house, you know, with a garden for Belle, and maybe a dog. Or do you think a little girl would prefer a cat?"

"I think we have plenty of time to decide, and, when she's old enough for a pet, Belle can choose for herself." Alex laughed and brushed his fingers through the baby's super soft hair. "Who knows, she might decide she wants a spider or a snake, or one of those odd little kinkajou things."

Damian straightened up and turned to look at Alex, disbelief in the tilt of his head. "A kinkajou? Really?"

"They're cute." Alex shrugged with a grin. He lifted Belle, one hand on her back, the other under her nappy-padded bum, and got to his feet. "Why don't we leave all this for a while and go out for a late lunch? You'd like that, wouldn't you, my beauty?" He bounced her and she made a happy, gurgling noise.

"You paying?" Damian asked.

Alex snorted. "You are such a cheapskate, Stanhope."

"Unless you've forgotten, *Jennings*, I no longer have a salary coming in."

"Aww, Belle, listen to your poor uncle, down to his last few million. However will he manage?" Alex's smiled widened with delight when Belle looked at him and actually seemed to be listening. It pushed aside the stab of unease he felt. He'd called the agency to take him off their books for the time being, so that he could help Damian with the baby, but the savings he'd had left after replacing everything when he came back from Africa were really starting to dwindle and he'd have to get back to work sooner rather than later. He knew Damian wouldn't hesitate to help him out if he asked, but Alex was uncomfortable with asking Damian for money, and he'd be damned if he'd give Grayson any reason to think he'd been right about Alex being after Damian's money.

"How about steak sandwiches at that place near Borough Market?" Damian asked, pushing his feet into a pair of flip-flops. He was wearing knee-length khaki shorts that showed off his strong calves, and a torso-hugging white T-shirt. His hair was a little longer than he normally kept it, streaked a couple of shades lighter by the summer sun that had bronzed his skin.

Alex's mouth suddenly felt bone dry and his dick shifted in his jeans. He could make a career out of looking at Damian. It wouldn't put food on the table, but, damn, he would put in all the unpaid overtime asked of him.

They settled Belle into her pushchair wearing the yellow sunhat her new Grandma Jennings had bought for her, and walked the short distance to the restaurant, pleased to see that the area was a bit quieter now that the Wimbledon fortnight was over. Alex's parents, living as close to the tennis club as they did, had always made a point of going on holiday for the two-week duration of the tournament to avoid the crowds. But this year they'd been reluctant to leave in case Alex and Damian needed them. Alex was certain his mother, who had never expected to have a grandchild of her own, was eager to swing into full granny mode, but Damian, as much as he loved and trusted Beth, was reluctant to let Belle out of his sight for now. Beth fully understood, but she'd been buying little outfits and toys and had encouraged Alex to take lots of photos of the baby for her.

"So, what do you think of the idea of a house?" Damian asked around a bite of his sirloin steak sandwich. "We could stop by an estate agent's on the way home and get some brochures. Or we could just look online, a lot of agents have really good sites now."

Alex swallowed his own bite of sandwich with some difficulty as unease twisted in him again. The truth was, until he got a full-time job, not just some locum work, he was in no position to co-sign a mortgage. He smiled, but his mouth felt a little stiff. "Sure, we can look."

"It's a buyers' market right now, with the economy in the toilet," Damian said, setting his half-eaten sandwich aside and reaching for his glass of sparkling water. "If we bought somewhere out of the city we could probably get a good deal. Maybe somewhere near Apollo's new stables; that looked like a nice town."

Alex remembered the property they'd seen the last time they'd been to see Apollo and he felt a little dizzy. They were talking high six figures at least. He coughed and took a sip of his own water to clear his throat. "We're not in a rush, so we can take our time and find the right place."

"I suppose the apartment will do for a bit," Damian said, clearly reluctant. "But it would be good for Belle to have her own room rather than a makeshift bedroom behind a screen in the living area."

That was true, and, now that they had all her things, it would certainly get cramped in the apartment. God, it used to seem so big and spacious. Alex made a non-committal noise because he didn't trust his voice not to crack with the pressure that was suddenly squeezing his throat.

Belle became a little fractious then, and Alex was grateful for the distraction. He took her bottle from the nursery bag, lifted her out of the pushchair and settled her in his lap to feed. He glanced at Damian from under his lashes and saw that his lover had pushed his unfinished sandwich aside and was turning his glass between his fingers, a frown knitting his eyebrows together.

Jesus, I feel like a prick. Alex knew he should tell Damian the real reason he was vacillating over the house, but he also knew that Damian would immediately offer to put up all the money and they'd end up in an argument because Alex was going to pay his own way, damn it. Hopefully, he would find a good job soon and they could start making serious plans for their future.

The walk home was made in a less than comfortable silence. They stopped in the market for some fresh-baked bread and pastries, and a selection of cheese, barely speaking half a dozen words to each other. Alex longed to take a detour past their favourite wine cellar and pick up a couple of bottles, but neither one of them was comfortable drinking while they had Belle to care for. He supposed that would pass in time and they would be able to open a bottle in the evening. But not this evening.

Belle was sleeping when they arrived home, so Damian carefully lifted her out of the pushchair, removed her hat and laid her down in her cot, shifting the silk screen around her to block out most of the light. As he watched, Alex saw — not for the first time — how gentle Damian was with the baby, and his heart swelled with fondness.

When he turned to find Alex watching him, Damian sighed and crossed his arms over his broad chest. "I'm sorry," he whispered.

Alex frowned. "For what?"

"You didn't..." Damian sighed again, clearly impatient with himself. He gestured to the screen behind him. "You didn't sign on for this. I've been so caught up in my own plans that I didn't even stop to think it might not be what you want."

Alex was so confused; Damian might as well have been speaking another language. "We're talking about the house, right?"

"The house, Belle." Damian shrugged, but it was as far from nonchalant as it was possible to be. "I know you love her, but I shouldn't have just assumed..."

Alex's spine stiffened as realisation dawned and his skin prickled with anger. "No, you're quite right. I didn't *sign on* for this." It was an effort to keep his voice low, but he didn't want to upset Belle. "I didn't sign on for anything; I fell in love, and, just in case you didn't know, that means being there for each other through the good times and the bad. The way Belle came to us was unspeakably cruel, but I adore her and I think she completes us."

"Oh." Damian's arms dropped to his sides and he looked adorably baffled. "But then, I don't understand. You seemed so against us getting a house, a family home."

"And you thought I didn't want Belle?" The anger left Alex on a rush of breath, and he moved closer to Damian. "You're an idiot, and so am I."

"Well, you're half right," Damian said, a little smirk kicking up one side of his mouth.

Laughing softly, Alex lifted a hand to Damian's jaw. "We're a partnership, right? Fifty-fifty, all the way?"

Damian nodded. "Of course." He was clearly still confused.

"The thing is, I can't... I don't..." Alex shook his head at his own stupidity. "I'm practically broke, love. I haven't worked in a while and I've been living off what savings I had. When we buy a house I want us to do it together, so if you could just wait a little while, until I get a job?"

For a moment Damian was silent, but Alex could see the laughter bubbling up in him in the way his blue eyes glowed and his lips twitched. "You're right, you *are* an idiot."

Smiling sheepishly, Alex leaned in for a kiss. "Yes, but I'm *your* idiot."

Chapter Twenty-Two

Lunch with Imogen at Covent Garden had become a semi-regular date. When Damian and Alex turned up one Thursday without Belle, Imogen's eyes clouded with disappointment.

"No munchkin?" she asked, looking around them as she unfolded her napkin, as if she thought they were hiding Belle.

Damian fidgeted in his seat, unable to get comfortable with the itch of anxiety crawling under his skin. He didn't realise he was tapping his fingers on the table top until Alex laid a hand over his and rubbed his thumb over Damian's knuckles. Damian smiled stiffly and tried to relax, but his stomach still felt unsettled. "Belle's spending the day with Alex's parents, probably being spoilt rotten." He laughed, mostly at himself. He knew he was being irrational; Belle was more than safe with Beth and Robert, who had taken to being grandparents with relish. Still, it wasn't easy for Damian to have the baby out of his sight for so long. It was all he could do to stop himself from calling to make sure she was all right.

"Darling, you're looking positively tortured," Imogen stated, eyes narrowing on Damian. She raised her hand to summon a waiter and requested the wine list. "You need to have a drink and calm down before you stroke out."

"I know I'm being stupid, but I can't help it." Damian shrugged. His apprehension didn't even make sense in his own head, but that didn't make it any easier to shake it off.

"Nobody thinks you're being stupid," Alex said firmly, squeezing Damian's hand. "Your concerns are perfectly reasonable. Have a drink with Imogen and I'll do the driving, okay?"

Damian nodded, and when he smiled this time it was easy, affection for the man beside him rolling over him like a wave.

"Oh my God, are you two for real?" Imogen made a gagging noise. "Please stop, I swore I was giving up sugar until I got into my new Donna Karan dress."

Alex grinned, and Damian leaned closer to him, fluttering his eyelashes adoringly.

Imogen snorted inelegantly, and when the waiter arrived with a bottle of chilled white wine she wiggled her fingers over her glass. "Fill it up, and keep it coming."

"Yes, ma'am." The waiter nodded and turned to leave, but not before taking the time to look down his nose at Damian and Alex's hands where they were still joined on the table, his lips twisting with distaste.

Imogen arched an eyebrow as he walked away. "Well, there goes *his* tip."

"Oh, I think we can come up with something better than that." There was a hint of devilment in Alex's tone that put Damian immediately on edge.

"What are you up to?" he asked, making no attempt to keep the suspicion out of his voice.

Alex smiled and leaned closer conspiratorially. "I'm going to teach you a little game I like to play with gentlemen like our friend the waiter. I call it 'let's fuck with the straight guy's head'."

In the hour that followed, Damian swung between fighting laughter and looking around for somewhere to hide. Every time the waiter came to their table — which was with inordinate frequency once Imogen caught on and decided to participate in Alex's game — Alex found an excuse to touch Damian. A thumb wiping away imaginary crumbs from his chin, fingers pushing a stray lock of hair off his forehead, straightening the collar of his shirt — all the while murmuring endearments like darling, love and sweetheart.

Damian had to admit he was grateful for the distraction they were offering, and he did find it fascinating to watch the waiter's complexion go from faintly pink to florid to explosive red. Part of him actually felt a little sorry for the tool when Alex *accidentally* dropped his napkin, reached under the table to get it and dragged his finger along the inseam of Damian's trousers, causing Damian to honest-to-god *squeak* with surprise. The waiter looked like he was about to swallow his tongue.

"You're a bad man, a very, very bad man," Damian accused, completely unable to maintain a stern expression.

Alex leaned in and rested his forehead against Damian's temple. "You have no idea," he half whispered, half growled, and Damian shifted in his seat again, this time to alleviate the sudden pressure in his trousers.

"Hey, hey, hey. Enough already. Sheesh." Imogen reached for her handbag. "I'll let you pick up the bill and you can consider it my payment for tonight."

Damian and Alex looked at each other and then at Imogen. "Tonight?" they asked in unison.

"Aww, how cute, do you finish each other's sentences, too?" Without waiting for an answer, Imogen threw back the remains of her wine and got to her feet. "I'll be at your place at seven to look after Belle. You boys put on your glad rags; you're having a night on the town. My treat."

"What? Wait..." Damian moved to stand, but Imogen shook her finger at him.

"Did you ever win an argument with me when we were married?"

A brief pause, and Damian shook his head. Imogen smiled. "Then why waste your time now? Seven o'clock. I'll be there, you be gorgeous." With a wave of her fingers she headed off.

Damian slumped back in his chair and turned to look at Alex. "I really didn't, you know, win an argument with her. Drove me fucking crazy."

"I bet," Alex laughed. "But it's a good idea, I think, us going out for the night?"

Damian wanted to argue, but the way Alex made it sound like a question stayed his tongue. Alex had been walking on eggshells for weeks now, worried about him, trying to hold everything together while Damian focused on himself and Belle. It was time to pay a little attention to Alex. Damian nodded and reached for Alex's hand. "Yes, it's a very good idea."

The smile that lit up Alex's eyes was nothing short of beautiful.

* * * *

When she said it was 'her treat', Imogen really meant it. She arrived promptly at seven and by seven-thirty Alex and Damian were in the silver Rolls Royce Phantom she'd hired for the occasion, on their way to a small, but very upmarket hotel in Kensington.

"Mr Stanhope, Dr Jennings, welcome to The Barrington." The receptionist looked like she could have been a supermodel, her perfect figure accentuated by an expensively tailored dark blue suit set off by a cream silk blouse. With her shiny, blue-black hair and friendly green eyes, she was just the type to have turned Damian's head not so long ago. Now, his entire attention had been irrevocably claimed by the man at his side. "Ms Fredericks told us this was a special occasion for you when she called, so we've put you in our Ambassador Suite. It has a lovely view of the city."

"Thank you, Sasha," Damian said, reading the name badge pinned to her lapel, rather surprised that she hadn't batted an expertly curled eyelash at two men booking in together.

Sasha smiled warmly. "Ms Fredericks asked us to reserve you a table in the restaurant, but also said you may wish to cancel the reservation in favour of room service. Our room service menu is quite extensive." There was clearly a question there.

Cheeks heating, Damian didn't know if he wanted to kiss or kill Imogen. "We'll let you know," he said.

"Well, the reservation is for eight-thirty and you'll find the restaurant on the top floor." Her mouth quirked a little at the corner. "You may wish to eat on the roof terrace. It's very romantic."

Alex wrapped his arm unselfconsciously around Damian's waist. "We might just do that, Sasha. Is there a dance floor?"

"There is indeed, and tonight we have a small jazz combo playing." She lifted a manicured hand to summon a porter and handed the young man a card key. "The Ambassador Suite please, David."

"Of course, Miss Blake. Gentlemen, this way, please." David moved ahead of them to the lift, pressed the call button, and stepped aside to let Alex and Damian precede him inside.

Soft music played as they rode up to the fifth floor. Damian and Alex stood close together, Alex's arm still around Damian's waist while Damian leaned into him. David glanced in their direction a couple of times and smiled knowingly, but it held none of the distaste displayed by the waiter that afternoon.

When they reached their floor, David led them along the hallway and unlocked a door, went inside and held the door open for them. "You should find everything you need, but if you have a particular request just call down and Sasha will be happy to help. Enjoy your stay at The Barrington, gentlemen." He handed the card key to Damian.

Damian took a twenty from his pocket and handed it to David, who smiled his thanks before he left, pulling the door closed behind him.

"Well, I'd say this was worth a lunch bill or two, wouldn't you?" Damian asked, coming to stand behind Alex in the middle of the room. He wrapped his arms around Alex's waist and buried his nose in his hair.

Alex laid his hands on top of Damian's where they rested just above his belt buckle. "I think we may need to buy Imogen diamonds for this."

The living room of the suite was decorated in shades of red and pale gold, with a high-gloss black coffee table between two plump sofas scattered with cushions. A large-screen TV hung on the wall and subdued lighting gave the room a very intimate atmosphere. Through an open set of double doors they could see a huge bed dressed in a ruby red throw, snowy sheets and a stack of pillows and cushions.

"Mm, maybe." Damian's attention shifted from the room to the soft skin of Alex's throat. "I don't want to talk about my ex-wife any more tonight. Right now, I don't want to talk about anything."

"Oh, really?" Alex tilted his head to the side, giving Damian more room. "And just what will we do while we're not talking?"

Damian lowered a hand from Alex's belt to curve it around his cock, feeling it swell and push against his palm. He nipped along the slight roughness of Alex's jaw, eliciting a soft gasp from his lover. "I have much better plans for my mouth." Alex offered no resistance when Damian manoeuvred him over to one of the sofas, turned him around and urged him to sit.

"You look great tonight." Alex reached out to touch Damian's shirt, trailed his fingers down to the fabric of his suit trousers. Damian's thighs trembled at his touch. "I've always loved you in all black."

Alex looked pretty damn great himself. The dark grey suit cut to perfectly showcase his wide shoulders and narrow hips, blue shirt stretched across his taut chest. Damian's cock stirred to life, swelling, filling rapidly at the sight of the man before him. He sank to his knees between Alex's legs and reached once more for his belt. They were both breathing deeply, anticipation heavy between them.

When he'd dealt with Alex's belt, Damian loosened his trousers and, with no preamble, dragged them and the shorts underneath down Alex's thighs. His dick sprang up eagerly, long and thick. Damian wrapped his fingers around the wide girth and his mouth watered. The first time he'd gone down on Alex, Damian had been hesitant and unsure. He couldn't imagine how sucking cock could be a pleasurable thing. The bittersweet flavour had taken a little getting used to, but he'd been enthralled by Alex's reactions, the way he'd writhed under him, the sounds and pleas that had spilled from his lips. There was little Damian enjoyed more now; the weight of Alex on his tongue, the texture and taste.

He dragged his thumb over the sensitive head of Alex's dick and smiled when he bucked his hips off the sofa.

"You want my mouth, don't you, baby?" Damian asked, sliding his fist slowly up and down the shaft. "You want to fuck my throat. You want me to squeeze your balls and tongue your slit."

"Holy fuck!" Alex pushed his hips forward, stretched his arms out along the back of the sofa. "Yes, Damian, do it. *Please.*"

Damian swept his tongue around the crown, added a hint of teeth to the ridge and heard Alex's cry of pleasure. He dipped lower, took in more, pressing his tongue to the underside so that Alex's cock rubbed against Damian's upper palate. When his lips met his fist, he pulled back off, cheeks hollowed out as he sucked. His own prick was pushing impatiently against the front of his trousers, and Damian had to resist the urge to rub against the edge of the sofa.

"Jesus, I love your mouth," Alex moaned. "So hot, so wet."

Damian moved his hand down to cup Alex's balls, rolling and squeezing while he lowered his head and took more of Alex in, stopping only when he felt the tip of his dick brush his throat. A harsh rush of breath left Alex, and, when he glanced up his lover's body, Damian saw that Alex had let his head fall back against the cushions, eyes closed, bottom lip caught between strong white teeth.

While Alex muttered praise and pleas, most of them barely coherent, Damian bobbed his head, sucking Alex in deep, flicking and swirling his tongue on the way up. He knew Alex was close, could feel it in the way his sac drew tight up against his body, but Damian didn't slow down, and as he continued to suck he released Alex's balls and reached farther back, rubbing his fingers over the smooth skin of his perineum.

"Fuck! Fuck, oh *fuck*!" Alex raised his hips off the sofa and seemed to freeze for a moment, and then he was coming, cock pulsing thick and bitter into Damian's mouth.

Damian didn't hesitate to swallow every drop. He couldn't get enough of Alex, and suspected that would never change.

When he pulled back after licking Alex clean, Damian looked at his lover, sprawled and wasted on the sofa, and his own cock, achingly hard now, throbbed between his legs. Alex opened his eyes and smiled lazily.

"That was... Fuck, there are no words." When he leant forwards it obviously took some effort. He cupped Damian's face between his hands and pressed a kiss to his lips. "What do you want?"

Damian sighed. "I want you to fuck me. I want to know what it feels like to take you into my body. But, first, I want us to go up to the restaurant and have a romantic dinner, and I want to dance with you."

Happiness glittered in Alex's eyes and he carded his fingers through Damian's hair. "That sounds perfect."

Chapter Twenty-Three

The roof terrace reminded Alex a little of the formal gardens at Garnet House. The tables were separated by topiary trees and neatly trimmed box hedges in terracotta containers, sprinkled with tiny points of white light. In the centre of the terrace was a water feature that looked like two ceramic urns, one sitting at an angle on top of the other, continuously trickling backlit water.

"Good evening, gentlemen. Welcome to The Terrace." The waiter, a young man in his twenties with an easy smile and hair like a surfer, handed them leather-bound menus. "May I recommend the slow-roast pork belly with plum sauce? It goes very well with a dry Riesling."

Alex handed the menu back without looking at it. "Sounds good to me. Damian?"

"You know, I would love a really good steak, thick, well done. Maybe chuck on some veggies to please Ma, and some red wine, whatever's good." He glanced up at the waiter with one of his most charming smiles, and Alex had to stifle a laugh when the young man blushed. "Could you do that for me?"

"That won't be a problem, sir. Can I bring you both some drinks while you wait?"

Damian looked across the table at Alex. "I'm thinking champagne... Too trite?"

"This *is* a special occasion," Alex said. He felt more relaxed than he had in weeks, and only part of that was owing to the spectacular blowjob Damian had recently given him.

A toothy grin made Damian look ten years younger and freer than he had in ages. "Excellent." His gaze lingered on Alex and the smile softened. Without breaking eye contact with Alex, he said to the waiter, "Do you have Bollinger?"

"We do indeed, sir. I'll be right back with that." The waiter slipped away, leaving them to their relative privacy.

"We can call this our first month anniversary," Damian said, reaching across the table to take Alex's hand. "We were kind of denied the chance to do all that mushy stuff."

Alex felt a rekindling of desire at the touch and moved his foot under the table to brush against Damian's. "We have years ahead of us for all that. Think of all the embarrassment we'll get to cause Belle when she's a teenager."

"Now there's something to look forward to." Damian chuckled and glanced around them. They weren't the only same-sex couple dining that evening, but Alex thought that none of the other men — or women for that matter — had anyone half so beautiful sitting across from them.

"This place is great," Alex said. "We really need to think of a way to thank Imogen."

"Hmm." Damian nodded and for a moment seemed preoccupied, but in the blink of an eye he shook off whatever had distracted him and he was back with Alex.

Alex squeezed his hand. "Belle will be okay with Imogen, you know that."

"What?" A puzzled frown creased Damian's brow, then understanding seemed to dawn and he smiled. "Actually, I wasn't thinking about Belle, I was thinking…well, it's not important right now."

"Trying to keep an air of mystery?" Alex asked with a cocked eyebrow and a smile.

Damian winked. "Make it worth my while later and I might spill."

"Oh, you'll spill. You'll also tell me what you were thinking about." Alex laughed, delighted at Damian's snort and the look of disbelief on his face.

"That was bad, Jennings, really bad."

The waiter returned with a bottle of champagne in an ice bucket on a stand. He opened the bottle and filled two long-stemmed flutes, and when Alex and Damian decided against any entrées, he dipped his head in a small bow and left.

"What shall we toast to?" Alex asked, holding up his glass.

Damian considered it, then grinned and clinked the rim of his glass against Alex's. "A toast, to toast, and how I will never kick you out of bed for eating it there."

It was a while before Alex could stop laughing long enough to take a sip from his glass. "Now there's a declaration of love if ever I heard one."

"Damn right," Damian retorted, eyes shining with amusement. "Part of the reason I divorced Gayle was that she liked to eat chocolate chip cookies in bed. Bloody crumbs got everywhere."

Dinner was every bit as good as the service, and, by the time they'd worked their way through the champagne and the wine that came with their meals, they had a nice little buzz going. Music drifted out from the restaurant proper, soft and mellow, and there was a singer who sounded remarkably like Lena Horne performing a rendition of *Summertime*.

Alex pushed his chair out, laid his napkin on the table and held his hand out to Damian. "You said something about dancing?"

"I did, didn't I?" Smiling, Damian took Alex's hand and got to his feet.

They made their way across the terrace and through a set of French doors into the restaurant. Alex made a move towards the small dance floor, but Damian paused, and Alex wondered if he'd had second thoughts. This was their first real date, the first time Damian had gone out with a man for romantic reasons. It was reasonable for him to be uncertain about being on display.

"We can…" Alex gestured over his shoulder towards their table, fighting down his disappointment.

Damian shook his head. "No, no, just give me a sec." He wound his way through the other dancers to the stage and whispered something in the ear of the piano player. When the man smiled and nodded, Damian gave him the 'thumbs up' and headed back to Alex, holding out his hand. "Shall we?"

Summertime finished as they stepped onto the dance floor and the intro to *Mad About the Boy* started. Alex rolled his eyes at a smirking Damian, but couldn't deny the thrill of pleasure that darted through him.

"So, who leads?" Damian asked, turning to face Alex, close enough that Alex could feel his breath on his cheek.

Alex placed one hand on Damian's upper arm and the other at his waist. "Nothing so formal. Just hold on to me and go with the flow."

"Hold on to you; I can do that." He wrapped one arm around Alex's waist, draped the other over his shoulder and they began to move to the music.

They were touching all along their bodies, temples pressed together, feet barely moving. It could hardly be called dancing at all, but for the gentle sway of hips. To Alex's mind it was perfect. He had the man he loved more than sanity should allow in his arms, Damian's heat and scent surrounding him, and one of his favourite songs in his ears; a veritable feast for the senses.

Damian's hand moved so that he could stroke the back of Alex's neck, drawing small circles with the tips of his fingers that sent shivers down his spine and raised goosebumps on his flesh. "This was a great idea," Damian said, soft as a whisper.

"Dancing?" Alex was starting to feel a little warm, and it had nothing to do with the ambient temperature. There was a persistent, low-level throb in his cock, and he could feel an answering pulse against his hip where Damian was pressed against him.

"All of it. The dancing, the night out, just you and me," Damian replied, then, after a brief pause, "I'm sorry, love."

Alex knew without asking what he was apologising for and he tightened his arm around Damian. "You have nothing to be sorry for. You're a good man,

Damian, and Belle and I are bloody lucky to have you in our lives."

A sigh brushed Alex's ear, and in that simple exhalation of breath he heard happiness, relief and contentment. He smiled and they lapsed into silence through *Stormy Weather* and *Ridin' on the Moon*.

When the first bars of *Just One of Those Things* sounded, Damian pulled back enough to meet Alex's eyes. "Let's go back to the room."

Alex arched his eyebrows. "No dessert?"

The smile that lifted Damian's lips was nothing short of feral. Lust hit Alex like a punch to the gut. He took Damian's hand and led him off the dance floor and out of the restaurant.

The ride down to their floor in the lift was made in silence. Nerve-tingling, pheromone-laden, electrically-charged silence. Owing to the presence of an elderly couple, they stood at a very respectable distance from each other, barely even exchanging glances; all very proper. The second they closed the room door behind them, however, respectable and proper hit the floor along with their clothes as they hurried towards the bedroom, a tangle of lips and arms as they tried to strip themselves and each other without actually breaking contact.

Alex's hands moved greedily over Damian, glorying in the smooth, bronzed skin before him. So beautiful... His lips followed his hands, trailed kisses down Damian's long throat, sucked on his Adam's apple. Damian's flavour burst on his tongue, salt and something citrusy.

"How could I have been so stupid?" Damian asked, so quietly that Alex wondered who he was talking to.

"Hmm?" He continued to walk Damian backwards to the bed while he nibbled along his collarbone and brought a hand up to scrape his fingers over Damian's nipples.

Damian's breath hitched when Alex leant down to suck one of his nipples into his mouth and his hand clutched at Alex's head, holding him close in a silent request for more. "I—I've been such a fool... Oh, God... We—we could have been doing this years ago."

"Don't." Alex lifted his head and met Damian's eyes, pupils fully dilated with need. "The past is gone. We can't change it, and dwelling on it will only steal time from our future."

Damian smiled, soft and fond, and brought his hand around to cup Alex's cheek. "Beauty *and* brains."

"Not to mention impeccable taste." Alex grinned and pushed Damian down on the bed. His eyes widened with surprise when Damian yelped and sprang back to his feet. "What the hell?"

Damian turned and Alex looked around him to see a box lying on the bed. It was about the size of a shoebox, decorated with shiny gold paper and an elaborately tied red ribbon. "That wasn't there earlier, was it?"

"I didn't see it. Maybe it was delivered while we were out?" Alex reached for the card tucked into the bow of the ribbon and a huff of laughter escaped him when he read it. *"Condoms are red, condoms are blue, they come in all colours and flavours, lube too!"*

"Imogen," they both said, laughing.

Damian tugged the bow free from the box and removed the lid. Inside were condoms in every colour of the rainbow and a selection of flavoured lubes.

"I may be shooting myself in the foot here," Alex said, his voice light with humour. "But why did you divorce this woman again?"

193

Damian chuckled and leant back against him. "It was a mutual decision. We both knew that we made much better friends than spouses. Thank God." He turned his head and pressed a kiss to Alex's temple.

"She's definitely a good friend to have." Alex reached into the box and withdrew a tube of strawberry-flavoured lube. "She gives the best gifts. Shall we try this?"

"For a starter." Damian moved the box to the floor and crawled onto the bed. When he reached the middle, still on his hands and knees, he looked over his shoulder. "Well, are you just going to stand there all night?"

Alex let his gaze roam over Damian, the curve of his arse, the arch of his spine, and the heat of desire in his blue eyes. Alex dragged in a deep breath and climbed up on the bed. "Oh, hell no. Beauty *and* brains, remember?"

Chapter Twenty-Four

A blend of apprehension and excitement seethed in Damian's stomach. He was far from being a blushing virgin, and after the last few weeks his confidence in bed with Alex had grown and got stronger. But the step he was about to take, as much as he wanted it, was pretty fucking huge. He felt a little like he was starting from scratch again.

The light brush of Alex's hand on his arse made him start, and he looked back over his shoulder. The expression on Alex's face as he trailed his hands over Damian caused his blood to rush hotly through his veins; it was all there, the love, the desire, the appreciation. He made Damian feel like he was the most beautiful thing Alex had ever seen. Alex's pupils were blown wide, and, as he ran the tip of his tongue over his lower lip, Damian's need flared, swamping his nerves until they were little more than a barely-there flutter.

"I'm going to take such good care of you, baby," Alex said, a hoarse whisper. He smoothed his hands down Damian's thighs and leaned in to place a kiss on his tailbone. A shudder ran through Damian and his dick stiffened, his fingers curling into the sheet when Alex dipped his tongue into his crack and swirled around his entrance.

"Oh, God, that's...more, please." Damian pushed back, and felt his hole wink at Alex.

Alex laughed softly, warm breath tickling Damian's most intimate flesh. "So polite. Who could deny such a well-mannered request?" He cupped and parted Damian's cheeks, and dragged the tip of his tongue from Damian's perineum to his opening, stiffening to push in a little way.

"Fu-uck!" Damian's breath hitched and his vision blurred at the pleasure that tore through him.

"We're just getting started," Alex informed him, reaching around Damian to grasp his cock, gripping the base in the circle of thumb and forefinger, squeezing just enough to keep Damian's incipient orgasm at bay.

Damian swallowed a moan and let his head fall forwards, and, *Jesus*, Alex's hand looked good on his prick. If he hadn't been holding Damian back, that sight alone would have been enough to make him come.

"You're a little on edge tonight, love. Pity Imogen didn't include a cock ring in her box of goodies." When Damian sucked in a breath at Alex's words, and his hole contracted again, Alex huffed a laugh. "Oh, you like the idea of toys, do you? I'll need to remember that."

Damian moved restlessly on the bed, spread his knees wider and braced a hand on the padded headboard. "Mm, wh—what kind of toys?"

"How about we start out with some dildos, open you up nice and slow, gradually getting bigger and thicker?" As he spoke, Alex pressed the tip of a lubed finger into Damian's hole, increasing the pressure until he was up to the first knuckle, then the second. He fucked in and out of him for a few moments before adding another finger. "Sound good?"

"Oh, fuck yes." Damian's voice was thin and breathy and a drop of perspiration rolled from the hairline at his temple to the corner of his eye. He turned his head enough to wipe it off on his shoulder. "Then what?"

"Hmm, maybe… Maybe once we've got you all loose and relaxed we can use a prostate massager?" He crooked a finger then, and Damian practically fucking *howled*, his grip on the sheet white-knuckled. Alex moved his fingers inside him. "Maybe one of those vibrating ones?"

"Shit. Fuck!" His head was buzzing, and his skin felt too hot, too tight. Who the hell needed toys when they had a lover with surgeon's fingers?

Alex eased his other fist up and down Damian's cock, and when he reached the head he pressed the tip of his forefinger into his slit. "Perhaps if you're feeling a bit more adventurous we could try some sounding rods?"

With a ragged, stuttered gasp, Damian shot his load over Alex's hand and the bed cover. His muscles turned to something like jelly and his elbows buckled. He collapsed, panting, on to his forearms, unable to hold his head up, arse still in the air.

Alex withdrew his hand from Damian's cock, brought it round to his rear and added the thick cum to the lube that was already there. With his other hand he stroked Damian's thigh. "Okay, baby?"

"Mmhm." Actual words were beyond Damian at the moment, as if the force of his release had fried vital synapses.

Cassidy Ryan

"You're all relaxed now; are you ready for me?" Alex was slowly rubbing his own cock on Damian's thigh. It was rock hard and leaking pre-cum freely.

The best reply Damian could give was to push his arse back at Alex. Oh yeah, he was so fucking ready; he had years of stupidity to make up for here.

In the silence that followed, Damian heard the soft snick of the lube being opened again, and then the vaguely obscene *slurp* as Alex slicked up his dick. It didn't occur to him to tell Alex to use a lot and be careful. He trusted this man with his life, and he sure as hell trusted him with his arse.

Alex was a big guy, though, and, as the head of his dick pushed past the first ring of muscle, Damian automatically tensed up. Alex immediately stopped and leaned over Damian's back to whisper in his ear, "Come on, baby, relax for me; let me in. Let out a big breath when I push in."

Damian took a few deep breaths and nodded, following Alex's directions. The pressure was intense, the sting sharp, and for a moment Damian thought he might panic. But Alex moved so slowly, murmured soft words of encouragement, and Damian gradually began to let go. When he reached back to take Alex's hand and nodded his assent, Alex pressed forwards once more.

It burned and it was uncomfortable, and his fingers curled into the sheet. He felt stretched past his limits and was sure his teeth were going to pierce his bottom lip. Then Alex bottomed out, the tip of his dick grazed Damian's prostate and, with a gasp of surprise, Damian felt his own cock twitch with renewed interest. "Oh!"

Alex stroked Damian's flanks, dropped kisses along the length of his spine. Damian could feel in the tremble of Alex's muscles the strain it was taking on his lover to hold back, and Damian moved his hips experimentally. Another jolt of pleasure shot through him and he realised that his body was beginning to adapt to accommodate Alex.

"Could you, uh, move...or something?" Damian asked, keen to explore the new sensations he was experiencing.

"You sure?" There was a noticeable quaver in Alex's voice.

Damian moved his hips again by way of an answer, and Alex groaned before withdrawing and pushing back in. With every stroke that followed, Damian's arousal increased until he was meeting Alex thrust for thrust, his cock once more hard and needy.

"Feels good...so good," Damian cried out. He grasped Alex's hand tighter and laced their fingers together. "More, love. Stop holding back, let go."

Alex didn't need to be told twice. His free hand gripped Damian's hip and he plunged into him, time and time again. Damian released Alex's hand, reached for his own cock and jerked it in time to Alex's strokes. Their moans and cries mingled, voices indistinguishable, bodies slip-sliding against each other. The tingle of orgasm began low in Damian's stomach and his hand sped up on his cock as his hole convulsed around Alex's shaft.

They came almost simultaneously with harsh grunts and muttered curses. The sounds of Alex's pleasure amped up Damian's release until he was sure he would pass out with the force of it, eyes losing focus, and, *shit*, it felt like his brain was going to *melt* and ooze out of his fucking ears.

Damian collapsed on the bed when his limbs refused to hold him up a second longer, and Alex slumped down beside him. He looked absolutely gorgeous; spent, wrecked. Damian reached out to push a damp lock of hair back off Alex's forehead. "Next time I want us to be face to face. I want to see what you look like when you come inside me."

"Next time?" Alex sounded as stunned as he looked.

Damian grinned. He was going to hurt tomorrow, no doubt about it, but it was totally fucking worth it. "I may never let you bottom again."

Laughter spilled from Alex's lips and he turned just enough to place a kiss on Damian's mouth. "We can wrestle for it; loser wins."

Damian laughed tiredly. "I've clearly spent far too much time with you, because that actually made sense."

"Beauty *and* brains, baby, your words."

"I'm going to regret saying that, aren't I?" Damian asked, chuckling. If he did, he was absolutely certain it was the only thing he would ever regret about this wonderful man.

* * * *

"So, what were you thinking about earlier?" Alex was lounging against the stack of pillows, Damian between his parted legs, back resting against Alex's chest.

Damian didn't even try to fight the grin that tugged at his lips. "Before or after '*Jesus Christ, is that a fucking baseball bat*'?"

Surprised laughter burst from Alex, and Damian felt the rumble of it through his body. "As flattering as that is, I was actually thinking about back in the restaurant."

"Oh, *then*?" Damian shifted slightly on to his right hip in order to look at Alex. It had the added benefit of shifting his weight from the not-totally-unpleasant ache in his backside. "I was thinking about this place, the hotel, and how it's the kind of place I had in mind when I put together my proposal for Stanhope Developments."

"And?" Alex arched an eyebrow, and Damian loved how he knew there was an *and*.

A sudden rush of excitement thrummed through Damian and he got to his knees in front of Alex. "What would you think about me doing this on my own? I'd need to review my financial projections and costings and such, update my lists of contractors, suppliers and designers, that kind of thing, but I've got a really good feeling about it. And I wouldn't be putting all my own money into it, so I wouldn't be risking our future. I still have a lot of contacts from my time at Stanhope; people more open-minded than Grayson who would love to invest in a project like this, though I'd be in overall control." He was out of breath by the time he'd finished.

For a long moment Alex was silent, and Damian's heart thumped uncomfortably quickly in his chest as he waited, hands resting on Alex's thighs. Then the corners of Alex's mouth began to lift and a wide smile lit up his handsome face. He reached out to take Damian's face between his hands and pulled him into a long, slow kiss.

"I think that's one of the best ideas you've had in a long time." The smile became a little mischievous then. "Not *the* best, of course, but it definitely runs a close second."

Damian's chest swelled with happiness, and without warning he launched himself at Alex, who squeaked in surprise before he flipped Damian under him and caught his mouth in a kiss that was hot and wet and deep. When Alex pulled away, Damian whined his disappointment, but it quickly turned into a moan when Alex kissed and licked his way down his body, stopped briefly to tongue-fuck his belly button, then moved on to suck Damian's rapidly hardening cock into his mouth.

Long into the night they drove each other to the edge and beyond, words of love and desire filling the darkness, and when they no longer had the higher brain function for words, they expressed their feelings through heated kisses and caresses until they were too exhausted to do anything but collapse in each other's embrace.

Chapter Twenty-Five

"Take us to Hatton Garden before we go home, would you? Do you know Bromley and Catz?" Damian directed his question to the back of the driver's head as he and Alex settled into the back seat of the Rolls.

"I do, indeed, sir." He pulled away from the front of the hotel, expertly manoeuvring the big car through Saturday morning traffic and jay-walkers.

"Why are we going to the jewellery district?" Alex asked as he stifled a yawn. He felt wonderfully used and rested, in spite of the lack of actual sleep they'd got the night before.

"I just want to pick something up." Damian laid a hand high on Alex's thigh and leaned in to whisper in his ear. "If this car had a privacy panel between us and the driver, I'd get on my knees for you right now. I'd open your trousers, take out that beautiful cock and jerk you until you were hard, and then I'd go down on you, suck you until you were a whimpering, writhing wreck."

"H—how very alliterative of you." Alex knew when he was being distracted, but when Damian spoke to him like that he found it hard to care.

"I'll let you hear some of my poetry some time." Damian grinned and settled back beside Alex, so close that they were touching from shoulder to thigh.

Alex laughed softly. "If any of it starts with 'There was a young man called Jock', I really don't want to know."

"Philistine," Damian muttered, and Alex was certain he heard a snicker from the direction of the driver.

Alex waited in the car while Damian went into the jeweller's shop. He was dozing to the soft music playing on the radio when Damian returned a little while later, looking very pleased with himself. Alex watched from hooded eyes as Damian took a long, slim, velvet box from a glossy black bag.

"What do you think?" He opened the box and Alex's eyes widened.

"Jesus, you actually bought Imogen *diamonds*?" Alex reached out and ran one finger along the sparkling bracelet, a sheepish smile lifting his mouth. "I was thinking flowers, maybe a nice box of chocolates."

Damian grinned. "I'm told good babysitters are like hens' teeth. I may want to whisk you away to Paris some weekend, so we need to keep her sweet."

It was on the tip of Alex's tongue to object to the expense when he was clearly in no position to contribute and Damian knew it, but, damn it, the man looked so fucking happy that Alex felt like he'd be kicking an over-excited puppy. First item on the agenda—get a bloody job. "She'll love it. But should I be worried that my boyfriend is buying his ex diamonds?" he teased.

Damian laughed loudly, as if the very idea was absurd, and Alex felt ridiculously pleased. He laced his fingers with Damian's. "Come on, let's go home and see our girl."

Imogen had more or less banned them from calling home, except in the event of an emergency. Alex had been concerned that Damian might spend the evening worrying about Belle; he liked to think he'd gone at least a little way to giving Damian something else to focus on.

The second they stepped through the door, however, Damian had eyes only for Belle. Alex shook his head, well aware that his expression was pure adoration, as Damian crossed to the living area and gently took his niece from Imogen's arms, bouncing her and cooing nonsense.

"Well, it looks like I am officially redundant." Imogen uncurled herself from the sofa and stretched luxuriously. She was wearing skinny jeans and a well-washed T-shirt, a marked departure from her usual sharp business suits. It was a good look for her.

Alex slipped off his jacket and dropped it on the corner of the sofa. "Everything okay?"

"She's a gem," Imogen said fondly, then winked conspiratorially. "Except at three in the morning when she wants to be fed and smells vaguely like the elephant house at the zoo."

Alex laughed. "Yes, the smell does take a little getting used to." He glanced over to where Damian was making silly faces at the baby and the laughter softened.

"You really are potty about him, aren't you?" Imogen asked quietly.

Alex's cheeks heated, but he made no attempt to deflect. "Both of them."

A slow smile curled her full lips and lit up her eyes. "Good. Now, how about some coffee?"

While Imogen went into battle with the coffee machine that seemed only to do Damian's bidding without drama, Alex collected the post from the table by the door, and, propping himself against the table, sorted through it. It was mostly bills and junk mail. Alex set the former aside to be dealt with later and tossed the junk in the waste paper basket.

The last letter in the pile caused his smile to slip when he saw the crest that identified it as being from the Stanhope family solicitor. He glanced over at Damian, currently playing a game of peek-a-boo with Belle, who clearly had no idea what was going on, but was grinning nonetheless. Alex would be glad when they got Romilly and Michael's estate settled finally. These constant reminders — not that Damian needed a reminder — usually left him quiet for hours afterwards.

"Come on, it's my turn." With a smile he hoped didn't look too strained, Alex went to Damian and Belle, holding out his arms for the baby while letting Damian see the envelope.

Damian sighed and dropped a kiss on Belle's forehead, then handed her over to Alex and took the letter. Alex lifted Belle up to his shoulder and gently patted her back, keeping his eye on his lover as he tore open the envelope.

The blood drained from Damian's face so suddenly that Alex wondered if he'd imagined it, then Damian slumped down onto the sofa as if all the strength had left his body. Alex was beside him in a second, one hand securing Belle to him, the other grabbing on to Damian's arm. "What? What is it?"

Damian's hand shook when he held up the letter. "It's... It's..." When he seemed incapable of speaking further, Alex reached out and took the letter from him.

"Alex? What's going on?" Imogen placed a tray of coffee cups on the low table in front of the sofa, concern evident in her voice.

He shook his head and quickly scanned the letter. Bile rose in his throat and his arm tightened around Belle. "Grayson... He's suing for custody of Belle."

"Oh my God, why?" Imogen asked, immediately going to sit beside Damian. "I thought he'd accepted this was what Romilly and Michael wanted?"

"He seemed to, when Susan spoke up about it at the will reading. I don't understand what's changed." Alex dropped the letter onto the table and brought his hand up to cup the back of Belle's head. Her hair was so soft it tickled his palm.

"Nothing's changed. It's the same old bullshit." Damian's voice was unexpectedly hard. He got to his feet and took his phone from his pocket. "Well, no more, damn it, *no more*."

Alex shook his head when Imogen sent him a questioning look. Anger boiled up inside him. Why would Grayson do this now? The man hadn't so much as picked up the phone to find out how his granddaughter had been in the weeks since the funeral. Susan and Hugh had called a dozen times and even asked Damian to sit Belle in front of a webcam so they could talk to her. What the hell kind of game was Grayson playing?

"Is he there, Helen?" Damian spoke into the phone. His tone was slightly softer, but there was a hard edge to his expression that Alex had never seen. Pride swelled in Alex—Grayson was going to have one hell of a fight on his hands if he really tried to take Belle from Damian. "No, Helen, I'm afraid everything isn't all right. But it will be. Yes, you take care, and love to Ma."

"Well?" Alex asked when Damian ended the call.

Damian's shoulders squared noticeably. "He's at the Belgravia house. I'm going to see him."

"Not alone, you're not," Alex said, taking a step forwards. For a moment it looked like Damian might argue, then he smiled, a small, barely there twitch of his lips.

"We're not taking Belle anywhere near him. Imogen, would you..." Damian didn't get a chance to finish. Imogen was beside Alex in an instant, reaching for the baby.

"Go and do what you have to do. I'll be here as long as you need me."

Alex smiled as he handed Belle over. "I might be a little bit in love with you, Imogen."

With a 'pfft' sound she waved him away, but her cheeks coloured slightly and she couldn't hide her own smile.

* * * *

Alex had never been to the house in Belgravia — when he'd left for Africa, Grayson and Naomi's London residence had been the Knightsbridge apartment that had also been the city home to Grayson and Lavinia. Alex supposed that Naomi had wanted somewhere without memories of Grayson's late wife.

The three-storey Georgian town house sat in a street of similar homes, meticulously maintained and smugly affluent. A butler — a fucking *butler* — showed them into a reception room decorated in stark white —

white walls, white furniture, white rugs on the hardwood floor. A chill ran through Alex. This was not a home for a child; it was a showpiece. He shuddered to think how Naomi would react to finding a sticky handprint on her pristine white sofa.

Damian paced the floor, hands tucked into his pockets, but far from casual. His lips were pinched in a tight, straight line and his forehead was scored with a deep scowl. He'd barely said a word on the fifteen-minute drive over, and the hands that gripped the steering wheel of his Mercedes had been white-knuckled. Alex had opened his mouth a few times to speak, but each time had said nothing. Sometimes words just weren't enough. He could only hope that Damian found some strength and support in his presence.

The door opened a few minutes after the butler left and Grayson entered, impeccably dressed in a suit and tie, even on a Saturday.

Every muscle in Alex's body tightened at the sight of the man and he experienced an urge to do something violent. He pushed his fists into the pockets of his trousers instead. He was here to help Damian, not make things worse.

"I won't pretend to be surprised by this visit," Grayson started, moving to the sofa, but not sitting — there was no way he was going to let Damian tower over him. "Let me just save us both some time. I'm not going to change my mind. I will not sit back and allow my granddaughter to be raised in such a thoroughly inappropriate environment."

It didn't escape Alex's notice that Grayson seemed to have decided to ignore his presence.

"Romilly wanted me to raise Belle. Didn't you hear what the solicitor said? It was her *greatest wish*."

Damian was seething, Alex could tell just by the set of his shoulders and the tightness in his expression, but he was clearly fighting to control his rage. "How can you, in all good conscience, ignore that?"

"Good conscience?" Grayson raised an eyebrow, and a small smile played around the corners of his mouth. "It was good conscience that urged me to make this decision. I have no doubt your sister loved you, and being the liberal woman she was I daresay she even approved of this...relationship you've got yourself into. I, however, do not."

"Love me, or approve?" Damian asked, a slight hitch in his voice. "No, don't bother answering that. It doesn't matter anyway. The only thing that matters is Belle."

"I'm glad we agree on that, at least," Grayson replied, and Alex's fists clenched tighter in his pockets. *You couldn't just tell him you loved him, could you, you bastard?*

"I'll fight you on this, Pa. I'll fight you every step of the way. I can afford good lawyers, too."

A look of condescending pity entered Grayson's eyes and he shook his head. "Ah, but you see, my boy, I can afford *great* lawyers."

Damian sucked in a deep breath and dragged a hand through his hair. "God damn it, you haven't asked to see her or even called since the funeral. This isn't about Belle, is it?"

Something unpleasant flickered in Grayson's expression. "This is about family, *my* family; past, present and future. I will not have my granddaughter raised by deviants and I will not allow you to taint the family line." His voice rose as he spoke and there was venom in the words and tone.

Alex bit down on his lip to avoid the retaliation on the tip of his tongue. *Deviants*? Jesus *Christ*, he loathed this man.

"You want to make a deal." Damian's voice was surprisingly calm. "I've seen you negotiate often enough to know the signs."

Grayson smiled, and damn if Alex didn't see a spark of pride in the man's eyes. He gestured between Damian and Alex with a dismissive flick of a hand. "End this travesty now, return to your family and the company and I'll withdraw my petition. You may be willing to give up your birthright for this man, but are you willing to give up Belle?"

The blood in Alex's veins ran cold at Grayson's words, and the glow of triumph in his expression was nothing short of ugly.

Damian, to his credit, didn't rise to the bait, although there was a definite sting in his tone when he spoke. "Your idea of family comes with too many conditions and strings attached for my taste. I want no part of it and I'll do everything it takes to protect Belle from it. Alex and Belle are all the family I want or need."

"Then, as they say, I'll see you in court." Grayson looked altogether too complacent. It filled Alex with unease.

Damian nodded. "Get ready for the fight of your life, Pa." He turned to Alex and gestured for him to precede Damian out of the room.

The butler was waiting in the foyer to show them out, and as they were leaving Alex caught a glimpse of Naomi descending the winding staircase. When she saw them she halted mid-step, her lips pursed, and rather pointedly turned and went back upstairs.

As he stepped out into the sunshine, a wave of nausea washed over Alex. He stopped on the front step and watched Damian stalking towards the car, stiff spine and clenched fists screaming the anger he had kept at bay in the house. Alex's chest tightened until it ached, his throat constricted and the backs of his eyes began to sting.

Belle couldn't be brought up in this place with those people. Her best chance for a good life was Damian, and Alex couldn't, *wouldn't*, jeopardise that. He knew without a doubt that Damian loved him, needed him, but he needed Belle more. There was always a chance they would win a court battle against Grayson, but Alex was certain the man would use every high-ranking contact and dirty trick he knew to swing the verdict in his direction. Damian had Romilly and Michael's wishes on his side, but that wouldn't count for much when Grayson's legal machine got going. They would use his relationship with Alex against him; turn it into something dirty and sordid.

A shaky breath escaped Alex and his heart felt like it was caught in a vice, twisting tighter and tighter with every beat. The only way to be certain Damian kept Belle was to give Grayson what he wanted, as much as Alex hated to admit it. Damian wouldn't, though; he would fight Grayson to his last breath and would probably lose anyway.

No, it had to be Alex. If Grayson was ever to leave Damian and Belle in peace then Alex had to remove himself from the equation. He had to leave them.

Chapter Twenty-Six

Damian turned over in bed and forced open eyes that felt gritty and heavy from lack of sleep. It had been well into the early hours before the adrenalin from his confrontation with his father had worn off enough to allow him to sleep, but even then it had been fitful, and now he felt thick-headed and drained. He managed to open his eyes enough to see that Alex wasn't beside him and that brought a smile to his lips. He was probably locked in round ninety-nine of his war of attrition with the coffee maker.

A soft mewling sound announced that Belle was awake and looking for attention. Damian pushed aside the covers and swung his legs tiredly over the side of the bed, hoping fervently that Alex had won this battle because he needed caffeine more than air this morning.

Belle's cries increased in volume as Damian left the bedroom and crossed the quiet apartment to the baby's makeshift bedroom. A frown creased his brow when he glanced in the direction of the kitchen and noticed a distinct absence of Alex. He lifted Belle out of her cot, tucked her favourite pink blanket around her and shushed her softly.

"Where's Uncle Alex got to, hmm? Ooh, maybe he went out to get some fresh pastries from that little bakery near the market? That would be lovely, wouldn't it?" As he spoke, Damian carried Belle towards the kitchen where he took the bottle he'd prepared the night before out of the fridge and placed it in the warmer. "I bet he went to buy coffee because he couldn't stand another defeat at the hands of our big silver friend. Maybe we can buy him a simple little percolator. I think he'd like that, wouldn't he?"

Belle's face was starting to scrunch up, heralding a full-out *bawl* if she didn't get her milk soon. Damian walked the kitchen floor with her, rocking her gently in an attempt to keep the tears at bay. It was on his third circuit that he noticed the keys sitting on the worktop. His footsteps faltered. "Looks like Uncle Alex forgot to take his keys. Wasn't that silly of him?" Something didn't feel right, and Damian had to force himself to cross the kitchen.

The keys were sitting on top of a folded piece of paper, and even without moving the keys he was able to see his own name scrawled in Alex's handwriting. Damian swallowed audibly and, with Belle secured in one arm, slid the paper out from under the keys. He unfolded it slowly, dread like a sliver of ice cutting into his heart.

Damian,
This is both the easiest and the hardest decision of my life. You'll come to see that this is the right thing to do. You can't lose Belle and God knows that little girl can't lose you. It will be easier for you to be together now. Let Grayson

have his victory, as long as you get to keep Belle. As you rightly said, she's all that matters now.

Take care of our girl and take care of yourself. I love you both.

Alex.

He stared at the note in disbelief as panic uncurled in his stomach and swelled until it seemed to press against his lungs, forcing his breath out in short, shaky pants. He was dimly aware of the ping of the bottle warmer letting him know Belle's breakfast was ready, but he couldn't seem to move. His limbs felt heavy and his head light. *This is wrong… This is wrong…* The words played on a loop and his fingers tightened around the note, crumpling it in his grasp. *Wrong.*

A plaintive wail from the baby in his arms startled Damian and he looked down to see her tiny fists shaking and annoyed colour touch her cheeks. He managed to move then, though he felt as though the air he was walking through was thick and resistant. With the ease of several weeks' practice he was able to test the temperature of Belle's milk without having to put much thought into it, and he headed towards the sofa where he balanced her on his lap and watched her latch eagerly on to the teat.

Alex was gone. He'd left them. He'd crept out some time in the night, believing that his presence placed Damian and Belle's future in peril. Believing his place in their life was less important. Beautiful, *stupid* man.

The ringing of the phone was another jolt to Damian's equilibrium, and, as if sensing her uncle's distress, Belle let the teat slip from between her lips and sucked in the kind of shuddering breath that usually came right before a bout of serious waterworks. He stroked her hair soothingly and coaxed her with whispered entreaties to take the bottle again, and when he was certain she'd settled down he reached for the phone, propped it on a cushion beside him and hit speaker. He wasn't expecting it to be Alex; that would be too much to hope for. He was right. It was Imogen.

"Morning, love, I just wanted to see how you guys are today?" Imogen had left fairly soon after Damian and Alex had returned the day before, staying just long enough to get the short version of what had happened, then leaving to give them the privacy they needed to discuss things.

Damian sighed deeply as exhaustion rushed back with a vengeance. "I think I may have fallen in love with the last honourable man on the planet." Even if that sense of honour was, on this occasion at least, foolishly misplaced.

"Uh, excuse me?" Imogen asked, she sounded sleepy and confused.

"He fell on his sword for us, Belle and me. Decided that we'd be better off without him." Tears stung his eyes and his voice fractured. "He's gone, Imogen; he left me."

There was a long silence, and Damian could practically *feel* Imogen frowning in confusion. "He *left*? No, that's… That's… Why would he *leave*?"

"Because my father is a narrow-minded, bigoted control freak and Alex clearly thought the bastard would call off the dogs if he thought he'd won." A surge of anger made Damian's head tingle, like a bad case of pins and needles. He took a couple of calming breaths and stroked his thumb over Belle's cheek. "Alex thought he was doing the right thing. He was wrong. And now I need to find him and tell him that."

"Which I'm guessing will be a lot easier said than done," Imogen said quietly.

"I don't even know where to start. He won't go to his parents', that's all I'm sure of. He knows Beth would tell me he was there." Fear twisted, sharp and sudden, in Damian's chest. What if he went back to Africa? What if...?

"I know a guy." Imogen's voice pulled Damian back from the brink of a thought that had the power to crush him.

"A guy?" he asked huskily.

"I was a tabloid hack for a while, remember? I have friends in low places, and one of them is a private investigator we hired to do some work for us. He specialises in the grey areas; nothing illegal, but morally questionable."

Damian had to smile at that. "Morally questionable; now there's a euphemism. You think he can find Alex?"

"Given the right incentive," Imogen replied. "A nice thick stack of twenty pound notes should do it, nothing traceable and certainly not taxable."

A flicker of hope ignited in Damian. "Whatever it takes, Imogen. Can you get hold of him today?"

"I'll do my best, love. You try to take it easy, okay?"

"I will. Call me as soon as you've talked to this guy, please?" He didn't try to keep the urgency from his tone. Imogen would never buy any attempt at casual, anyway.

With Imogen's promise in his ears, he ended the call and turned his attention to Belle. She'd sucked down two-thirds of the milk and spat out the teat, now more interested in playing with her toes. It occurred to Damian that she should be in desperate need of a nappy change by now, but she was dry and decidedly un-smelly. His breath caught on a sob. Alex had taken the time to change her before he'd left. He'd stopped by Belle's cot to say goodbye to her.

Stupid, *beautiful* man.

* * * *

By the end of the week Damian was ready to scream, pull his hair out or both. He was tired to his bones, head and neck aching from the tension gripping his body and, with every passing second that failed to bring news from Imogen's investigator, his anxiety hitched up another notch.

Imogen had been a rock, making sure Damian didn't spend too much time alone, and listening to him when the fear and pain refused to be contained any longer. He'd finally given her the bracelet a couple of evenings before, and, even though she'd cried in her gratitude, it had felt woefully inadequate for everything she'd done for him.

A week. Alex had been gone for a week, and Damian felt like he was slowly and quietly losing his mind. Imogen had contacted her guy and he'd agreed—for a price—to track down Alex, but the bloody man was proving to be as elusive as the Scarlet fucking Pimpernel.

Not surprisingly, Belle was refusing to settle, no doubt picking up on her uncle's agitated mood. Damian had tried laying her in her cot to see if she would sleep, but her fussing didn't abate, and when he picked her up, rocking her and making soft shushing sounds, she seemed only to get worse, her own restlessness apparently amplified by closer proximity to Damian.

When he felt ready to snap, the walls pressing in on him claustrophobically, he put Belle in her pushchair, tucked his phone into the back pocket of his jeans and left the apartment. Ten minutes into their walk along the river, Belle was sound asleep and Damian could feel the breeze blowing away some of the fuzziness in his head. He stopped in a cafe for a bacon sandwich when the grumbling of his stomach reminded him that he hadn't eaten since the few bites of chicken tikka masala he'd ordered in the evening before, and lingered over a pot of tea.

"It gets better, love."

Damian lifted his gaze from the cup of tea in front of him and blinked a few times at the waitress standing beside him. "Excuse me?"

An indulgent smile touched the woman's lips. She looked like she was in her fifties, and reminded Damian a little of Martha. "Parenthood. I've been through it four times myself and I recognise the signs of sleepless nights. I swore to God mine were the devil incarnate sometimes, when they kept me up all night, but when you see them like this you forget all about that." She looked at Belle sleeping soundly in her pushchair, one small hand curled up beside her face, the picture of innocence.

Some of the weight in Damian's chest lifted and he smiled. "I plan on getting my own back. You know, white socks with sandals, showing her friends how to dance *properly* at her first boy-girl party, asking very loudly in the supermarket if she needs tampons, that kind of thing."

The waitress laughed and patted him on the shoulder. "You'll do okay." She was still laughing softly as she drifted off to serve another customer.

Damian finished his tea, left a tip on the table and manoeuvred the pushchair out of the cafe, heading home. He felt a little less on edge on the journey back, but the silent phone was still a heavy weight in his pocket.

At the front door to the building he was punching in the access code when a shadow fell over the keypad. Damian turned, and his frown turned to surprise when he saw Jude, his father's driver, with a manila envelope in his hand.

Damian's hackles rose. "Doesn't he pay solicitors a ridiculous amount of money to deliver bad news?"

"Your father didn't send me, Damian." Jude's expression was unflinching. He tapped the envelope against his thigh. "In fact, I'm no longer in his employ."

Damian's eyebrows rose, back to surprise. "You're not?"

One wide shoulder lifted in a shrug. "I know he's your father, but the man is a prick. What he's doing...he shouldn't get away with it." Jude handed over the envelope, and, without another word, turned and left.

Damian watched until Jude disappeared down the street and around the corner, then looked at the envelope in his hand. "Well then, that wasn't weird or mysterious at all." He finished putting in the code and went inside.

Once inside the apartment, Damian carefully moved Belle from the pushchair to her cot. She scrunched up her nose and smacked her lips a couple of times, but she didn't wake and quickly settled again. He opened the envelope, and, finding a computer disc inside, went to the office and started up his laptop.

The disc contained a dozen files, and, as he opened and scrolled through each file, Damian's emotions ran from shock to disbelief and rage, and finally relief so overwhelming that it took his breath away.

He was so engrossed in the information on the screen in front of him that it took a minute to register the ringing of the phone. When the sound eventually did make an impact, Damian jumped out of his seat and wrestled the phone out of his pocket, almost dropping it twice before he managed to hit *accept*. "Imogen!"

"We've found him, Damian," she said without preamble, her voice higher pitched than normal with excitement. "We've found him!"

Damian's knees gave out and he slumped back down into his chair, tears of elation blurring his vision. *Thank God.*

Chapter Twenty-Seven

Being back in London was making Alex feel antsy. The city was huge and the chances of accidentally bumping into Damian in a coffee shop in Notting Hill were miniscule, but he was still fighting the urge to look over his shoulder every few seconds. He'd spent most of the last week just driving aimlessly. Heading south when he left, he'd found himself in Brighton, where he'd spent the night before going west along the coast, only stopping when he'd felt the need for food or to stretch his legs, or when the view had been so particularly stunning that he'd had to get his camera out and take some pictures.

He'd run out of money around Plymouth, and, faced with a choice between the camera and the car, he'd sold the car and continued his journey by bus. When he'd reached Penzance in Cornwall he'd turned north, and just yesterday he'd been in Wales. He'd called his parents from a call box in Tenby, having turned off his mobile phone to avoid having to ignore Damian's calls, and the stab of guilt he'd felt at the worry in his mother's voice lingered in his chest now.

"You can't stay away forever, Alex," she'd said.

"I don't need to stay away forever, mum, or even for very long. Just long enough for Damian to realise that this is the best thing for him and Belle."

"He's been calling," Beth replied, and Alex could hear the tears in her voice. The knife in his chest twisted. "I'm worried about him; I'm worried about both of you."

"I know, Mum, I know. But this really is for the best, I promise." Why did he feel like he was trying to convince himself as much as his mother?

He'd thought about going back to Africa, had even gone as far as calling the agency to learn that they had negotiated with the local government there to ensure the safety of returning aid workers. But in the end Alex couldn't bring himself to make a commitment. He'd left Damian and Belle, but found he couldn't leave the country completely. Of course, the resurgence of the nightmares over the last few nights might have had something to do with his reluctance.

A heavy hand on his shoulder made Alex jump and yanked him roughly out of his thoughts. His head snapped around and he found himself looking into the warm brown eyes of Martin Collins, the man who'd been his superior and mentor when he was training to be a surgeon.

"I'm not sure if that's relief or disappointment I see on your face, my boy." Martin grinned, his round face as open and friendly as it had always been. He took the seat across from Alex's, wincing slightly as he sat. "Too many years on my feet in operating theatres; the old legs are just about ready for the knacker's yard."

For the first time in a week, Alex felt a genuine smile lift his mouth. "You know I'm always pleased to see you, you old rogue."

"I'd say less of the old, but the grey doesn't lie." He dragged a hand through brown hair now liberally sprinkled with strands of silver. "Still a handsome bugger, though."

Alex laughed. "Ah, if I was twenty years older…"

"You'd still be twenty years too young." Martin chuckled. It was an old joke between them. He'd been happily married, if unofficially, to George for over thirty years now.

"How's that poor, long-suffering man of yours?" Alex asked, attempting to catch the eye of a waitress.

"He's a grumpy, crotchety old fart, but he's still as flexible as a teenage gymnast, so I'm happy." Martin's smile was mischievous, and Alex snorted.

"You're incorrigible." Alex waved the waitress over. "A refill for me, please, and the largest cappuccino you can come up with for my friend here."

"Lots and lots of chocolate sprinkles, my lovely," Martin added with his most charming smile. When the waitress went to get their order, he turned back to Alex. "Now, perhaps you'll tell me why I had to arrange a meeting with you through your mother? You're not on the run from the law, are you?"

This time when Alex laughed it sounded hollow. "Of course not. I took a little impromptu holiday and decided to turn off my phone, that's all." He turned his gaze from Martin to the street beyond the window.

"So, you *are* on the run then. Who is he?" Martin asked.

Alex shifted in his seat, suddenly uncomfortable. He shook his head and his throat tightened with emotion. "I don't… It's complicated."

Martin sighed. "Matters of the heart usually are, my boy. Is it anyone I know?"

The waitress returned with their drinks and Alex had a precious moment to gather his composure. He was *not* going to have a meltdown here, damn it.

Martin was watching him expectantly when they were alone again. Alex shook his head and smiled in spite of the ache in his chest. Stubborn old bastard.

"You remember my friend Damian?" he asked.

Martin's eyes widened almost comically. "Damian Stanhope? Blond, beautiful and never far from a leggy female?"

"That's the one." *Jesus*, just the mention of the man's name hurt.

"Well, how about that then." Martin looked genuinely surprised. It wasn't an expression Alex was used to seeing on his old mentor's face. "I believe I met his father once, at one of those infernal fundraising events. Bombastic, self-satisfied fellow, if I recall."

"Don't get me started." Alex didn't even try to keep the bitterness out of his tone. "I'm sorry, Martin, but I really can't talk about this right now."

Martin must have heard the ragged edge to Alex's voice, because, even though his curiosity was shining in his eyes, he kept it to himself. "You know where I am if you need to talk. Now, why don't I tell you why I interrupted your holiday?"

"Please do." Alex smiled gratefully and reached for his cup.

"Well, George and I have decided *that* time has come; we're retiring. We've found a place we want to buy in France, near Saint-Malo. It comes with a small vineyard and enough gourmet restaurants nearby to keep us fat and happy for many years to come." Martin stirred his cappuccino, and Alex couldn't miss the hint of excitement in the man's expression.

"That sounds wonderful, Martin, congratulations." If anyone deserved a chance to kick back and relax for a while it was Martin. One of the finest general surgeons in the country, Martin was now creeping up on seventy and had postponed his retirement at least three times that Alex knew of at the pleading of a hospital board desperate to keep him on staff.

"George and I still have a few good years left in us, and, at the risk of sounding mawkish, we want to spend them together." Affection for his partner was bright in his eyes.

Alex couldn't help feeling a little envious. What would it be like to grow older and deeper in love with Damian? He quickly shouldered the thought aside. It was bad enough that he cried like a lovelorn teenager in private; he sure as hell wasn't going to do it here. He raised his cup to Martin. "It's not champagne, but I wish you and George all the happiness in the world."

"Thank you, my boy. Now, the hospital board, understandably devastated by my imminent departure"—he winked at that—"have decided that, instead of advertising and interviewing for my successor, I should be the one to appoint my replacement. That's where you come in."

"Me?" Alex asked, confused for a moment, then his eyes widened in understanding. "*Me*? You're offering the job to *me*?"

"I can think of no one better," Martin said, his tone rich with sincerity.

All the air left Alex's lungs and he slumped in his chair. Consultant General Surgeon at one of the best hospitals in the UK. He'd wanted a good job, but *damn*! "I don't know what to say."

"Well, unless you plan on saying no, I'd like you to start as soon as possible, work side by side with me for a while to make the changeover as seamless as possible for everyone involved." Martin scooped a spoonful of chocolate foam off the top of his coffee and swallowed it with a sigh of pleasure.

Alex laughed, stunned. "No wasn't a word that immediately sprang to mind. This is an amazing opportunity, Martin, I'm...floored."

"How soon can you start? Because the sooner you start, the sooner I can leave. I'm rather looking forward to a life of indolence."

When he left the coffee shop an hour later, a little over-caffeinated, Alex had agreed to start work the following Monday and promised to have dinner soon with Martin and George. He took the Tube to Euston station and walked the short distance to the budget hotel he'd booked into the previous night. It wasn't The Barrington, but it was clean and cheap, and, right then, cheap was a very big selling point.

The hotel lobby was crowded with tourists; a cacophony of chatter in more languages than Alex could count or understand. He worked his way through the melée to the blessedly quiet lift and took it to the sixth floor, where the only sound was the creaking of the floorboards under his feet. The lock on his door refused the card key twice before it finally allowed him in. Alex shook his head and pushed the door open, only to freeze on the spot.

"I was going to kick your arse for the week you've just put me through, but by the looks of things you haven't fared any better." Damian got up from the chair in front of the Formica-topped desk and came towards Alex. Even with the dark circles under his eyes and the tired slouch of his shoulders, Damian was still the most beautiful man Alex had ever seen.

Chapter Twenty-Eight

The blood drained from Alex's face so suddenly that, for a second, Damian thought the man was going to pass out. He took another step forward, just in case, but stopped when Alex flinched. The door was still open behind him, and Damian wondered if he was actually going to turn around and run.

Instead, Alex seemed to just sag. He moved further into the room and closed the door, tossed the card key onto the dresser. "You shouldn't have come here, Damian. How did you get in, anyway? And how did you find me?" With each question his frown deepened a little further.

"Did you really think I'd just let you leave like that, Alex? Did you think I *could* let you leave and do nothing about it?" Damian wanted nothing more than to go to him, to touch him, but Alex was standing stiffly, arms crossed over his chest. "I've been looking for you since I woke up alone. I didn't like that, Alex, waking up alone. I never used to mind, but now..."

"I suppose you batted your eyes at some poor chambermaid and conned your way in here?" There was the tiniest hint of a smile playing around Alex's lips. It gave Damian heart.

He shrugged. "People want hard cash these days. We live in ugly times."

"Well, it doesn't matter, I suppose. Nothing's changed." Alex's arms dropped to his sides and he leant back against the dresser. He looked as tired and drained as Damian felt. His eyebrows pulled together, and a flicker of panic crossed his features. "Where's Belle?"

Damian smiled and a surge of energy rushed through him. "She's spending the day with Grandma Beth and Grandpa Robert."

"She is?" Alex looked adorably confused.

"She is," Damian confirmed. "Because you and I have an appointment to keep."

"We do?" And the adorable just kept coming.

Damian's heart swelled with affection and he could no longer fight the urge to touch. He lifted his hand, trailed the backs of his fingers down Alex's cheek. A sigh escaped Alex and he leaned into the caress. "Damian..." It was barely more than a whisper, but so filled with longing that it made Damian's heart twist.

"I've missed you so much," Damian said, turning his hand to cup Alex's cheek. He leaned closer, inhaling Alex's scent, and it was like an electrical charge to his senses. God, this man made him feel *alive*. "Where have you been?"

Alex brought his hand up to rest on Damian's chest, over his heart. "Lost," he answered, voice husky, eyes overly bright.

"Oh, bugger it." Giving himself no time for second thoughts, Damian reached out with both hands and pulled Alex into a tight hug, slamming their bodies together so that he could feel his lover stamped all along the length of him. He felt Alex's brief hesitation before he put his arms around Damian and he was clutching at Damian's shirt.

"This is stupid," Alex said, voice muffled by Damian's shoulder. "He'll take Belle. *Nothing's changed*."

His anguish tore at Damian and he crushed Alex to him for a moment before pulling back so that he could look into his eyes. "You're wrong, love, *everything's* changed."

"What? I don't understand."

Damian stepped back and took Alex's hand. "You will, later. But right now…" Without another word, he tugged on Alex's hand and led him over to the bed. With a ragged intake of breath, Alex let himself be led.

They stopped by the side of the bed and, when Alex lifted his hands to the front of Damian's shirt, Damian could feel that they were trembling. Damian laid his hands over Alex's and bowed his head until their foreheads were touching. "I had thought to sweep in here and ravish you," he said, smiling.

Alex laughed. "Have you been reading Jane Austen again?"

"Actually, I thought of myself as more of a Heathcliff type." Damian smoothed his thumbs over Alex's cheekbones and breathed deeply of his scent. God, it felt so good, so *right*, to have this man in his arms.

Alex turned his head and placed a kiss on Damian's palm. "Well, don't let me stop you, my Heathcliff. Ravish away."

Giving no warning, Damian hooked his leg around Alex's and tumbled him to the bed. Alex yelped in surprise, but his eyes were glowing with amusement. Damian's body tightened with need and his blood felt like it was on fire. He slipped one knee between Alex's legs to rest on the edge of the bed and lowered himself on top of Alex. "I'd rather be your home," he whispered.

Alex's eyes widened. He raised himself up on one elbow and wrapped his other hand around Damian's neck. "You've always been that." The kiss he pressed to Damian's lips was like an exclamation point.

Heart thumping violently in his chest, Damian deepened the kiss and let his full weight rest on Alex, wanting to feel as much of Alex's body as possible. Lips parted, mouths opened and tongues tangled as they fed on the taste of each other until they were breathing harshly. As he dragged his mouth along Alex's jaw and down his throat, nipping and biting lightly, Alex wound his legs around Damian's thighs and tilted his hips up so that Damian could feel the hard swell of his cock.

Damian groaned and rested his head against Alex's shoulder. His hips seemed to move of their own accord, pushing into Alex, grinding their clothed erections together. Their rough, needy groans filled the air, unreserved, uncaring of who might hear.

"Fuck, Damian!" Alex's back arched and he clutched at Damian. There was a sound like fabric ripping and springs creaking.

Damian felt hot enough to burn and he strained against Alex, his hands gripping the sheet on either side of Alex's head. "Alex...fuck, I-I...too *long!*" His hips snapped once, twice, and a low, breathless growl escaped Damian. Fierce pleasure tore through him, and, when he felt Alex stiffen and shudder under him, it seemed to heighten the sensations to almost unbearable levels.

They lay wrapped around each other for some time, simply breathing and touching. When he was finally able to feel his limbs again, Damian pushed up to rest on his elbows. He looked down at Alex and his heart swelled at the unabashed love he saw reflected there. "My home," Damian said in a hushed voice, and Alex smiled. Damian leant down to brush his lips against Alex's ear and laughter bubbled up in his chest. "I doubt Heathcliff ever came in his trousers."

Alex's laughter rumbled through them both.

"Where are we going?" Alex asked, picking up his speed so that he was keeping pace with Damian as they left the room an hour later and headed towards the lift.

"We're going to see my father." At Alex's gasp, Damian smiled. "I promise it will be more...productive this time."

Alex continued to look baffled as they rode down in the lift and hurried to Damian's car, parked at the back of the hotel. When they were seated, Damian reached under his seat and withdrew the envelope Jude had given him, now thicker with printouts of the files, and handed it to Alex. "Here, you might find this interesting." He started the engine, pulled out of the car park and turned the car in the direction of Belgravia.

For a while the only sound in the car was that of Alex flipping through the documents. His presence at Damian's side was like balm to Damian's soul. He reached over and laid a hand on Alex's thigh, needing a physical connection.

"I don't believe it," Alex finally said, sliding the papers back into the envelope. "This is...oh my God!"

Damian nodded, eyes narrowing as he turned the car into Grayson's street. "Indeed." He drew the car to a halt in front of the house, switched off the engine and looked at Alex. "Ready?"

Lifting Damian's hand, Alex brushed the knuckles with his lips. "Oh, hell yes."

They were shown into the same reception room as before by the butler, Stockwell, and soon afterwards joined by Grayson.

"This is becoming tedious, Damian," he said, his expression one of boredom.

"Is Naomi home?" Damian asked, ignoring the way his father rather pointedly checked his watch.

Grayson frowned at that, clearly puzzled. "No, she's out shopping, why?"

"Because I don't think you'd want her to hear what I have to say." Damian gestured to one of the hideous white sofas. "You may want to have a seat."

"Oh, just get on with it, boy. I'm a busy man; I don't have time for this nonsense."

Damian bristled at Grayson's tone, his eyes narrowing. "Fine, I'll dispense with the niceties and get to the point. You're going to drop your petition to gain custody of Belle, and while you're at it you're going to sign a document giving your support to Alex and me legally adopting her. I have the paperwork here, just to save you a trip to your solicitor. Stockwell can witness your signature."

Surprised laughter burst from Grayson. "Oh, really? And just why would I do this?"

Damian took a step closer to his father, opened the envelope and withdrew the contents. "Because, along with the legal documents, I have a few others that might be of interest to you. Like this, the address of the apartment you bought for your mistress." He held out the paper, which Grayson snatched from him. Damian's hand trembled slightly with resurgent anger as he removed a photograph from the bundle. "Or this picture of the two of you in a rather...passionate embrace."

"Where the hell did you get this?" Grayson demanded, colour rising in his face.

Damian snorted, the sound more disbelief than amusement. "Yes, Pa, because *that's* the important thing here; not the fact that you're fucking my ex-wife."

"Mind your tone, boy," Grayson retorted, but there was little of the usual force in his voice.

"I'm not going to ask when you started with Shannon, because, frankly, I don't care. Does Naomi know about Shannon?" The slight twitch of Grayson's eye was all the answer Damian needed. "No, I didn't think so. She'd have you in the divorce courts before you could say *offshore accounts*, and she'd take you for everything. I'm actually more interested to know if Shannon is aware of your Thursday afternoon meetings with Felicity at the Mayfair corporate apartment?"

Grayson did sit then, all colour bleeding from his face. Damian felt no sense of triumph; rather, a flicker of sympathy ignited in him. But he ignored it; he had to see this through to the end. It was the only way.

"Ready to sign those papers yet, Pa? Or maybe you're willing to face Naomi's wrath? And let's not forget Will; I'm sure he'll have something to say about all this." It was harder to go in for the finishing blow than Damian had expected, but he stiffened his spine and shoved down his reluctance. "How about the board of directors at Stanhope? How do you think they'll react to this mess? What was it you said to me when Alex and I got together...? '*In the current climate a scandal like this could be disastrous.*' I'm inclined to think they'll oust you in a heartbeat, but you might have a different opinion."

In the silence that followed, Damian could practically see the wheels turning in his father's head, reviewing his options, trying to come up with a counter plan. Damian knew it was over when Grayson sighed tiredly, got to his feet and turned to Alex. "Perhaps you would be good enough to ask Stockwell to join us?"

Alex nodded and quietly left the room.

"Blackmail, Damian?" Grayson asked when they were alone.

Damian shrugged. "Leverage, Pa. I had a good teacher."

There might have been a spark of admiration in Grayson's eyes, but it was gone too quickly for Damian to be certain. "Is there anything else you want before we tie everything up? A kidney, perhaps, or my head on a platter?"

"Now that you mention it, there are a couple of things." Damian dropped the envelope on the coffee table and tucked his hands into the pockets of his trousers. "You fired me for being in a gay relationship. We both know that if I took you to an employment tribunal I would win, so you're going to pay me severance commensurate with my years and position in the company."

Grayson nodded. "Go on."

"This is more for the long term. Whatever would have come to Romilly and me when you pass will now go to Belle, including Garnet House. Naomi is more than welcome to this place, but Garnet House is Belle's." Damian made sure his tone let Grayson know this was a deal breaker.

Again, Grayson nodded. "That's acceptable."

Alex came back then, followed by Stockwell, and, as Grayson and the butler signed and co-signed the documents that would secure Belle's future, Damian took Alex's hand and felt the weight of the last week finally lift. It was enough to make him feel lightheaded.

"I'd say it was nice doing business with you," Grayson said, handing the signed paperwork to Damian while Stockwell quietly excused himself. "But we both know I'd be lying."

Damian shook his head sadly. "See, Pa, that right there is your biggest problem. You saw this as just another bit of business. If there comes a time when you want to stop being just a businessman and want to be a grandpa, let me know; maybe we can work something out." He turned to Alex and the unabashed love shining from the man's eyes stole the breath from Damian's lungs.

"Are you all right?" Alex asked when they were back in the car. "I know that couldn't have been easy for you."

Damian smiled and leaned across to press his mouth to Alex's in a soft kiss. "Better than all right."

"I'm glad you didn't close the door completely on Grayson." Alex lifted a hand and cupped Damian's cheek, smoothing his thumb over the skin under his eye. "Everybody deserves a chance to redeem their mistakes."

Damian took Alex's other hand between both of his. "I'm not holding my breath, but you never know. Now, enough about Grayson. He's taken enough of our time and attention lately."

"I'm sorry I left the way I did, but I really believed I was doing the right thing. You know that, don't you?"

Alex's eyes pleaded with him to understand and Damian's heart twisted.

"You did it for Belle and me, so, however misguided it was, I get it. Why don't we go and get our girl and go home?"

Alex smiled and there was an edge to it that made Damian arch an eyebrow in question. "My things are still at the hotel. I haven't checked out yet."

Damian's pulse kicked up a notch and sudden heat invaded his body. "Oh, really?"

"This may be completely inappropriate, but…you were magnificent in there and I am unbelievably aroused right now." Alex moved Damian's hand so that it was resting on the hardness pressing against the front of his trousers.

Damian sucked in an uneven breath. "You are, aren't you? In that case, it would be a shame to waste a perfectly good hotel room. I daresay your parents won't mind Belle's company a while longer."

"They'll be in their element," Alex replied, pressing Damian's hand closer and moaning his pleasure.

Damian's own cock stirred to life and he shifted in his seat. "Babe, if I'm going to drive us anywhere, I'll need my hand back."

With gratifying reluctance, Alex released his hand. "Put your foot down. I'll pay for any speeding tickets from my fabulous new salary."

Damian's head snapped back round and he grinned. "You got a job?"

"I did, and I'll tell you all about it later. Now would you *please* start the damn car?"

Laughing, he did as he was told, but before he moved the car he closed the distance between them and claimed Alex's mouth in a brief, hard kiss. His love for the man felt so immense that Damian wondered if his heart could possibly contain it. "This is going to be so good."

From the gleam in Alex's eye, Damian knew he understood that Damian was talking about much more than an encounter in a hotel room.

Alex laid a hand on Damian's thigh and smiled. "The best, love, the best."

About the Author

Cassidy Ryan lives and works in the West of Scotland, with Angel, the not-very-angelic kitty.

When she isn't writing, Cassidy enjoys football, shopping for the perfect handbag, main-lining coffee and watching TV.

Cassidy Ryan loves to hear from readers. You can find her contact information, website details and author profile page at http://www.total-e-bound.com.

Total-E-Bound Publishing

www.total-e-bound.com